Resurrectionists

The Iowa Short Fiction Award

Prize money for the award is provided by

a grant from the Iowa Arts Council

Resurrectionists

RUSSELL WORKING

UNIVERSITY OF IOWA PRESS

IOWA CITY

University of Iowa Press, Iowa City 52242

Text and jacket design by Richard Hendel
Typesetting by G & S Typesetters, Austin, Texas
Printing and binding by Braun-Brumfield, Ann Arbor, Michigan

The publication of this book is supported by a grant from the
National Endowment for the Arts in Washington, D.C.,
a federal agency.

Library of Congress Cataloging-in-Publication Data

Working, Russell, 1959–
Resurrectionists.

I. Title.
PS3573.06926R4   1987   813'.54   86-30754
ISBN 0-87745-164-8

Contents

Charis 1

Resurrectionists 23

Shooting 53

Rendering Byzantium 61

Pictures of Her Snake 107

The Monkey 115

Famous People 137

On Freedom 149

Charis

3
CHARIS

To the best of Len's recollection, he met Charis on New Year's
morning, just after two o'clock. There had been a party. He
remembered talking to her. The crowd had finished the last of
the champagne, and Len had an image now of a corpulent
drunk (someone he knew from work, maybe) sprawled unconscious on the couch, mouth open, a red party hat crushed
beneath his head with its string cinched under his jowls. Len
knew that as he went for his coat he bumped into her, a tall,
striking blonde in a black dress, whom—he was now becoming increasingly convinced—he had spotted through the
crowd but had not had the opportunity to meet. Did he intro-
duce himself? Did she toss back her hair and smile beautifully
and perhaps say, "Pleased to meet you, Len. I'm Charis"? He
remembered her mentioning she had noticed him earlier,
"But you were so deep in conversation I left you alone." She
said, "You remind me of someone I used to know." "Who is
he?" Len asked. "Nobody, really," she said. "He died in an explosion at an aluminum plant down in Longview." "I often do
that to people," Len said, "remind them of someone."

Later, as he tried to piece together what had happened, he
found to his vague interest that his memory not only of the
previous night but of significant portions of the preceding
year was blank.

Len asked, "Did we eat dinner together?"

"No."

"But there was a New Year's party. Somebody kept blowing
a whistle in my ear."

"Yes. At Sean and Julie's. Do you remember who they are?"

"Of course."

Charis twisted the watch around her wrist. "I don't mean
to be rude."

He shrugged. "I know I spent the night at your house."

"A couple hours of it."

Len set aside the steel rack so the plastic tube would not
bisect her face.

Charis said, "You shouldn't lift that."

"Why not? What do you want me to do, ring for a nurse?"

"I'd be glad to do it."

"Thanks, I'm not paralyzed." The man in the next bed looked at Len, and Charis smiled at the bed rail. Len considered his reflection in the television screen on the wall against the ceiling (his hospital-issue pajamas open on his wiry chest; arms at his side, one palm upturned and the other down; his hand inserted with a three-inch-long, pliable needle connected to the intravenous tube), and he decided that even unshaven and messy-haired, lying in a cagelike bed, he was not an unattractive man.

He ventured, "And we made love?"

"Don't you remember?"

"Yes, of course. I'm just stating the things I recall."

"I thought it was a question."

"No, it wasn't." Actually, the only thing he could remember was an electric blanket that had been turned too high, but he did not wish to be undiplomatic.

Charis asked, "Do you remember the paramedics?"

"No."

"You were sitting on the edge of the bed talking to them. You were quite lucid—funny, in fact. They asked you what drugs you had been taking, and you said, 'Cocaine.' You pointed to the table in the kitchenette and said, 'There's a whole bowl of it in there.' The one paramedic got up and looked at it with his eyes bugging out and said, 'Good heavenly days! What's the street value of this? $20K?'"

"I took cocaine?"

"Um, no. You were kidding him. It was the sugar bowl."

"Oh."

"I guess he was pretty naive. His partner, the woman, was laughing. She said he came from this Missouri Synod Lutheran family who owned an apple orchard near Wenatchee."

"Huh."

Charis said, "Do you remember anything else?"

"Not much."

"Do you remember my name?"

"Of course. Charis."

They laughed. Charis stood up and patted his arm. "I've got to go," she said, and then, digging in her purse as she walked to the door, "I'll drop by this evening." Len called, "You don't have to," but she was gone, clicking down the hall in her high heels—a dry, aberrant sound amid the padding of the nurses' white sneakers, as if her heels were made of bone.

Len groaned and began adjusting the angle of his bed with the electric controls—bending the knees, a little higher, then back down a bit, raising the back—until he was positioned like an astronaut awaiting launch. There was a sensation he wished to alter in his back, legs, arms, buttocks, and neck. He considered the sensation and its name. He ached. He felt as if he had spent a day pitching bales of hay onto a flatbed truck. Then his eyes were closed and he knew he had slept, but he wished to keep them closed and think. Periodically he awoke and lay like this, or the nurse woke him and he opened his eyes and put capsules in his mouth and drank a glass of water. He attempted to recall what he could of the party and what had happened, and by the time the nurse brought his dinner tray he had recovered several fragments, shards of memory to dust off with a camel's hair brush and tag and classify. The older memories of the past year, he saw with relief, were returning of their own accord.

Charis had awakened him in the middle of the night and asked, "How are you now?"

"What?" Len groaned.

She was leaning over him and pressing his cheeks between her hands, her breasts hanging in her diaphanous nightgown. Traces of mascara ringed her eyes, and her blonde hair was tangled. "How are you doing?" she whispered. "Are you all right?"

"I suppose so, considering I've had maybe an hour's sleep."

"You just had a seizure."

"What?"

Charis' chin quivered. "You stiffened, and you thrashed around kicking and woke me up. You drooled all over the place. I can't believe how strong you are. Your fingers were fanned out, and I couldn't even squeeze them together."

"A seizure?"

"Yes."

"Oh, my head hurts. Maybe that's it. I thought it was the champagne. Hey, how come I'm all wet?"

"I tried to bring you out of it by dashing a cup of cold water in your face."

"Did it work?"

"No. You nearly drowned until I rolled you onto your side."

"Oh."

"Do you want to get back in bed?"

Len looked around. He lay on a hardwood floor, wrapped in a twisted rope of sheets, beside a heating vent. A tuft of dust dithered in the warm draft. He climbed into bed. Charis collapsed on the mattress beside him and brushed his hair from his eyes.

"Do you have epilepsy?"

"No."

She touched his belly. "Maybe I should call a doctor."

"No, don't," he yawned and fell asleep.

Sensing the motion of a vehicle, Len lifted his head long enough to survey his torso, lying flat on a raised bed, draped with a blanket (a red cross on the blanket: an inverse Swiss flag), and foreshortened like a painting in a Spanish cathedral of an interment, only reversed, viewed from the head. The pink-and-emerald lights of a marquee (TONIGHT ONLY: Two for one after Midnight HAPPY NEW YEAR!!!) swept his body and disappeared in the silent cruising of the van. He asked, "Did I tell her about it?" "Shhh," said the woman in the blue jacket. Len asked, "Wasn't there someone else who could do that?" "Yes," she said, "I'll tell you who later." Relief overwhelmed him, and he lay back.

Light suffused an entire field of vision and intensified into a sun moving here and there, burning green zigzags on his retina, yet a voice like that of a man said, "Don't look at the light. Watch this. Wherever it goes, I want you to follow it with your eyes."

Len looked and in an act of will caught sight of a fleshy blur a few inches from his eyeballs.

"That's right. Just watch my finger. Good." And then distantly the man said, "I guess it's all right to let him go now." The pinpoint of light and the finger went away, and several young women in white unstrapped the canvas bands binding his ankles, knees, wrists, elbows, and chest. Len was dressed only in a canary yellow pair of briefs whose fly was printed with a caricature of Satan and the words "I'm a little devil." He blushed and looked around for his clothing.

"Don't struggle or we'll tie you back down," said an Oriental in a white coat who tugged on a wispy vandyke. He asked, "Do you have epilepsy?"

"No."

"What drugs were you taking last night?"

"None."

"You sure?"

"Yes."

"What's your name?"

"Len Demarest."

"Good." The doctor helped Len sit up and asked, "Do you remember your address?" Len repeated a sequence of numbers and letters that seemed familiar, while the nurses watched, the broad-faced one, a black woman, chewing on a pen. The doctor nodded at his clipboard. "Do you know what happened to you this morning?"

"I had—" What was the word? Somewhere a synonym

rattled a cup against its cage, but Len silenced it: "I had a seizure."

"You had three of them. Grand mal seizures. Two at your girlfriend's place and one in the ambulance."

Then the doctor asked a dozen other questions, kneaded Len's neck, prodded his scalp, knocked on his knees with a rubber hammer, did everything but shake a talisman and attempt to suck the demon from his patient's head, and finally said, "Well, I think this should do," and, scribbling on his clipboard, "Mr. Demarest, we'd like to keep you here several days for tests. We need to get to the bottom of whatever's causing this. I've got you on Dilantin now, and that should keep you from any more convulsions for the time being." Convulsion, thought Len: explosion, implosion. The doctor sniffed and left the room, followed by the nurses.

Len's clothes had been wadded up and tossed on a chair against the wall, and he glanced at the door, then hopped from his stretcher, snatched up his pants, and struggled to pull them on. The room reeled and he balanced himself by holding the rail of the stretcher while his pants dropped to his ankles. A black nurse entered and said in surprise, "Oh."

Len pulled up his trousers and climbed back on the stretcher with them still unbuttoned. He lay down. The nurse introduced herself. She had an unusual accent and said she was from Montreal. "Pleased to meet you," said Len.

The nurse said, "For a moment I thought you were dressing so you could sneak out on us."

Len inched toward the head of the plastic surface, which clung to his back, and said, "No. I wouldn't make it to the front door, let alone back to my apartment. Not without help, anyway."

She laughed and pushed his stretcher out of the room.

Len's parents arrived just after Charis departed. His mother rushed in and kissed him, laying a bouquet of roses wrapped in green plastic on his chest, and his father opened one eye wide and comically arched his eyebrow and shook Len's hand. "They treating you all right?" he inquired. Mrs. Demarest's face was puffy and red from crying, but she began arranging the flowers in a vase on Len's dresser and asked, "Now, who is this Charis you were with? Somebody I ought to know about? She sounded very nice when she spoke to me on the phone this morning." Len said, "I don't know." She winked and said, "Oh, come on." "No," Len said, "I really don't remember." Mrs. Demarest plucked a dead leaf and opened her mouth to protest, but when she saw his expression, she took the vase over to the sink and filled it with water and said nothing.

"Mom."

"Yes," she said, her back still to him.

"Do you remember the story about the mining camp that Aunt Carla told us when she got back from her vacation to South Dakota?"

"Honey, Aunt Carla hasn't been back to South Dakota since she came to Seattle in 1941 to work at Boeing."

Mr. Demarest said, "Yes, she has. What about that trip?"

"Hal, she only got as far as Missoula before she had her first heart attack and they had to fly her back. You remember."

"Mom, wait. On that trip, didn't she say something about people mining for gold in a graveyard?" Len's father was pacing the room, nodding once at the patient in the next bed. Len said, "It was in a town in the Black Hills."

Mrs. Demarest set the vase on his dresser. "I don't remember that story."

"Yes," Len said, then cut himself off.

Mr. Demarest paced the room and squinted with his glass eye at the posters on the wall (the only one Len could see advertised a production of *Tannhäuser*) until Len realized what was the matter and turned on the Rose Bowl game. The Huskies were playing Michigan. Len's father sat and gripped the armrest of the chair and said with relief, "First quarter."

Charis did not come that evening—not while Len was awake, at any rate. He dozed but fought to rouse himself; he dreamed he was shaking his head, slapping his face, rolling out of bed onto the floor, and still his eyes would not open. He dreamed about the whiteness of his room. The nurse woke him for dinner. "Your parents said they'd be back to-morrow," she said. Afterward Len chatted with the man in the next bed, Cal, a middle-aged patient whose gray hair was matted in locks and draped across his balding head. Cal said he was an accordionist.

Len said, "Professional?"

"Sure."

"Where do you play?"

"Lots of places: dances, parties, clubs. I even played at a wake once. Don't laugh; they paid well. It followed an open-coffin funeral for this beautiful sixteen-year-old girl with a figure that would knock you dead, and everyone was so senti-mental they kept requesting her favorite pop songs and stuff-ing bills in my tux pockets." Cal grew distracted and stared out the window beside his bed.

"What are you in here for?" Len asked.

"I'm paralyzed from the neck down. I got a little movement in my right hand that I think is getting better. See me twitch my fingers? Pretty exciting, huh? The doctors can't figure out what the hell is causing my problem. Probably a tumor or something in my brain, just like you, I guess. That's why we're in neurology. I told them to crack my skull open and have a look round, but the sons of bitches won't do it. They say it's too risky."

As Cal spoke, Len recalled a joke he had made to Charis, and he winced and clutched the sheet with his toes. Then he asked, "Is there much of a view over there? I can't see very well from here."

"Nah. Just the other wing of the hospital and some damn sculpture."

Len tried to think of something to say, but Cal muttered, "Would you mind if I closed the curtain between our beds? I'd like to get a little shut-eye."

"No," said Len.

Cal bit like a snapping turtle on a piece of plastic tube that bent around from behind his bed, and the curtain buzzed on its track and encircled his bed.

The next morning there was no sign of Charis. Len was slightly nauseated when the orderly brought his breakfast, and he ate only half an apple that was browning on his plastic tray. His mother dropped by for half an hour, then departed, saying she would be back that evening, after his father got home from work.

At twelve-thirty Charis arrived, carrying a canvas bag and a thermos.

"Want to sneak out of this place?"

"Sneak out? What for?"

"I don't know. I thought we might take a ride on a ferry, have a picnic somewhere, something like that."

"I don't think I could get past the nurses' station."

"Sure you can. I asked them if you could join me for a cup of coffee in the cafeteria now that you're off of the intravenous fluids, and they said okay."

Len laughed and glanced at Cal, who shut his eyes. "All right. Can you slip my clothes out for me? They're hanging in the closet."

"Sure. These?"

"Yeah."

"They look familiar."

"Right. Similar to what I wore the other night."

As they walked past the desk, Charis slipped on her sunglasses and grinned at the black nurse with the broad, familiar smile. She looked at the thermos. "Enjoy your coffee," the nurse said. "Thanks," Len called.

They drove to the terminal below the Pike Street Market on the waterfront and caught a ferry to a small island in Puget Sound. The sky was pale blue over the dark sound, and cirrus clouds streaked the southern horizon. To the west the Olympic Mountains were stark and icy above the hills and evergreens. Later Len remembered drinking tea while they stood on the balcony at the bow; he was unsure where they had gotten it. He pinched his tea bag and scalded his fingers. Charis mentioned the cold port wind, and he turned his collar up. A gull hovered low over the wake alongside the ferry; it seemed to be slipstreaming. Len flung his tea bag in the sound. The gull lunged at it as it fell steaming to the water but missed, fell away, and circled back to look for it. Charis bit her lip. Len watched her and tried to remember something (a dream, maybe, about the open front of a ferry, with cars parked on the pavement that slipped over the green scudding sea), but when she glanced at him the sensation vanished.

"Beautiful," Charis said.

"Pretty nice weather for January."

"It is. Can you believe it snowed last week?"

"Oh."

"You remember? It might have been the week before that."

"Did we do something that day?"

"No. Well, I'm sure we did, but not together."

"Of course not. Silly me. We didn't even know each other then."

Charis gave him an odd look. Her nose was turning red in the cold, and he suggested they go inside.

After landing at the island's dock, they walked along a road that curved southward, past scattered wooden houses with moss growing in fistlike clumps on the shingled roofs, until they came to a grassy park that sloped to a boat dock and a clear, pebble-strewn marina. They sat at the sunny end of a picnic table beside a tilting Douglas fir that was oozing sap. They were on the leeward side of the island, and the air was still and brisk and smelled like salt and turpentine. They removed their coats—Charis was wearing a sweater and skirt, Len his tuxedo jacket and ruffled shirt and slacks (one leg of which was crusted with cheese dip, which he had elbowed from the table while impersonating Richard Nixon at the Kitchen Debate). Charis opened her bag and spread out a tablecloth, on which she set a loaf of rye bread, sausage, cheese, fruit, and a bottle of wine.

She handed him a napkin and said, "Dig in," and then Len saw he had missed something and she was repeating, "Have they figured out what's causing those seizures?"

"Not yet. They'll be testing me tomorrow: EEG, CAT scan, the works. They ought to figure it out. And they say they have medication that completely controls these things, so no matter how it turns out I'll be as good as new. I'm on something now. Dilantin and something else."

"Good. Have some wine."

A mallard waddled about a few yards away in the shallows, watching them. As they finished eating, Charis tossed a scrap of bread to the bird. The mallard gobbled it and stared at them with its thumbtack eyes. Mallard drakes always reminded Len of the simple toys that children build from sets: a bill inserted in the green-black head, a ring like a washer separating the head from the neck, a squat body that made you want to punt it like a football, and flat feet. A group of ducks out on the water began quacking and paddled closer. "They're hungry," said Charis.

Len dipped a piece of bread in his wineglass and tossed it out to the water's edge. The pink scrap crumbled in two, and the ducks squawked and fought over the pieces. The drake got one fragment, and a hen snatched up the other. They turned up their bills and shook their heads and tried to swallow the bread, and the flock parted and chased the two until they managed to choke their bread down.

Len and Charis laughed. He put his arm around her. "They love it," she said, "here, give me that loaf." She tore off a piece of crust, dipped it in wine, and flung it underhand to the birds. They flapped and fought each other. A drake emerged from the melee and gulped the scrap on the run.

Len and Charis roared with laughter. They crumbled hunks of bread, soaked them in wine, and threw them to the ducks. The birds wobbled about nipping each other and flapping their wings. Two drakes pursued another out over the water, tipping the surface with their feet until they got airborne; they swooped crazily and chased the other bird back to another part of the bank, where they pounced on it and nipped at its feathers. Two mottled hens fought over a pink rock until each had bit it; then they wandered in opposite directions. Charis giggled and swigged her burgundy. Sometimes a duck would stumble to the shallows and stoop to fill its bill; it would raise its head and bob its throat and gulp down the salt water. Down drifted along the shore.

Charis said, "That's enough. Look at them, the poor things!"

"Just one more for the big guy."

"Don't, he's drunker than the rest—he ate half the bread. Stop it." She tried to grab Len's wrist.

"One more," said Len, tossing the scrap to the mallard. The bird gobbled down the bread, then weaved its way up the beach before collapsing. It thrashed about and beat its wings on the pebbles, then opened its mouth and heaved, jerking its head forward.

"Jesus!" said Len.

"The poor thing," said Charis.

Len tiptoed toward the bird, but before he reached it, it fled flapping across the water. A green feather stirred on the bank. The mallard paddled to the dock. The rest of the ducks shook themselves and quacked at Charis as she packed the leftovers in her bag and dumped the remnants of their wine on the trunk of the fir. They never got to the coffee. Instead they returned to the terminal and caught the next ferry back to Seattle.

As the ferry approached the Seattle terminal, they again stood at the bow on the second level. The sun was setting behind them, and the wind was bitterly cold, but they leaned on the rail and watched the drivers returning to their cars below and revving their engines. The dark green water boiled against the oil-stained pilings, and a group of men on the dock unhooked a chain and prepared to lower a ramp to the car level. Len and Charis reentered the overheated interior and stood among the crowd of people rustling about buttoning their sweaters and coats.

Len said, "I feel strange."

Charis took his arm. "What do you mean?"

Out of an infinite number of inquiries and arrangements of words, she chose to toss out the one that was tied like a millstone around his neck—and although Len, Leonard, Leonardo, I immediately forgot the question, what horrified him was the sea into which her words sank him (couldn't she have chosen other means?) or, rather than a sea (outside, though skin is porous), an implosion of white dread: Len, do you need to sit down? Wasn't there a crowd that pressed us at that level too, backs puffy in their winter coats? Listen, come over here and sit down, Len. Didn't the window fog as we looked out on the churning green-white froth? Are you going to be sick? Whispering, do you want me to help you to the bathroom? Len! Didn't this attract the interest of a crowd with stale chewing gum breath while our muscles tingled and cramped? As if a fluorescent tube exploded (the particles of glass sting and prickle the skin), something flashed.

Pressed back against the windows and chairs along the walls as Len reached down, the people laughed. A man with a scruffy beard lifted his backpack from the floor (unaware that the bellyband still hung, bright orange, to the ground) and said, "Well, that's one way to clear a crowd away from the exit." They laughed again. Our tormentors required that we hang up that instrument: the one with the keyboard and collapsible structure: saying—"Len," she said. "Please. Can you understand me?"

"Can you understand me?" asked the redheaded man with a crust of acne around his nose, his face pockmarked. He wore an embarrassingly bright yellow shirt (perhaps there had been a tie like that, painted with a nude woman, which someone found around his neck when he woke up in the presence of ladies). He was finished with the light.

"Yes, doctor. Len Demarest."

"Almost. It's Glen Demarest."

"What?"

A nurse whispered and pointed at the clipboard.

"Oh, I'm sorry, you're right. It's Len. Can't read the handwriting here. Now, I'm going to mention three things, and I want you to remember them and repeat them when I ask. Think you can do that? Great. Listen carefully: lightbulbs, the color red, and Park Place. Now, where do you live?"

Len recited an address.

"You got the address right, but this is Seattle."

"What did I say?"

"You said Geneva."

"I went there on vacation last summer."

"Good. I'm glad you remember that. Okay, can you tell me those three things I asked you to remember?"

"No."

"Come on, now. Try."

"I am. I can't remember."

"Very well." The doctor made a note on his clipboard.

Len said, "Where is—where is she?"

"You mean your friend?" The doctor scowled. "I haven't the slightest. She evidently told the paramedics she would follow them here in her car, but she must have gotten lost in traffic." He whispered to the nurse, then added aloud, "I ought to just leave you tied down there," smiling. "Seriously, I hope you won't try to slip out of here again, Len. You know, you're in here of your own free will. If you want to check out and leave, nobody will strap you to your bed. But I trust this afternoon has convinced you of the importance of these tests we're going to run. We've got to find out what is the matter with you."

"Yes, I know."

"Good. It's about time you understood the seriousness of all this."

A black nurse entered Len's room and spoke in a melodious accent. Her laugh was deep, and she was short and busty and rather overweight.

"Where are you from?" asked Len, and she laughed.

"Do you want anything else?" she said.

"No, thanks. Nurse? I guess I had another seizure."

"Yes, you did."

"On the ferry."

"Yes."

"What happened?"

"We haven't talked to your girlfriend yet, but the paramedics said it hit you while you were getting off. I guess she knew a little better what to do this time. She said this one man yelled at her to stick her fingers in your mouth to keep you from swallowing your tongue, but she told him to shut up."

"Why was I naked when I woke up here?"

"Um, your clothes were wet. They undressed you in Emergency."

"Wet?"

"It seems that after your seizure you unbuttoned your pants and urinated on the floor, and you got it all over yourself."

"Ah. In front of everyone?"

"I don't know who all was there. I think probably no one saw it except your girlfriend."

"She's not my girlfriend. I doubt I'll ever see her again."

"Oh. I beg your pardon."

"That's all right."

"At least she won't try to sneak you out again. That was very bad of you—both of you."

"Nurse? Wait a second."

"Yes?"

"Uh, do you know her name?"

"Whose, the lady you were with?"

"Yes." Len looped the plastic tube over his elbow, out of the way, and sat up with a groan. His muscles ached. He saw his reflection in the television screen. "I forget her name."

"I'm not sure. It might be in your file."

She left the room. A few minutes later, as she was walking past carrying a bedpan, she stuck her head in the door. "Charis," she said.

"That's an unusual name," said Len.

"I know. I never heard it before."

"What's your name?"

She shook her finger at him. "You'll just have to remember; I'm not telling you."

As people entered his room, Len awoke from a dream, only a fragment of which he could remember: he was carrying a golden, bejeweled orb through an alley that stank of rotting meat, but the orb kept slipping through his fingers and rolling behind piles of waxy cardboard boxes or under dumpsters. A tall, lean doctor nodded at him, but the others walked straight toward the curtain without a glance at his bed. One man held the curtain open as the others entered Cal's part of the room, then himself entered, and the cloth draped back in place. Someone spoke, his voice muffled, low, and uneven, like a tuba heard through the walls of a practice room.

Len clicked through the channels of his television set with the remote-control button. Cal's voice sounded indignantly: "Permanent! What the hell do you mean, permanent? When I came here they were saying a couple months, maybe three, and I would be better. I thought you had surgery that could fix me up."

Two doctors spoke at once. A voice won out, but Cal shouted it down: "I don't give a damn if I can go home! Are you saying I'll never be able to play the accordion again? That I'll have to have a nurse to wipe my ass for the rest of my life? I'm fifty-eight, damn you; I can't live another twenty, twenty-five years like this."

A doctor spoke, and the nurse flung aside the curtain and trotted from the room. The voice was soothing, but Cal sobbed: "God, this is ridiculous. I can't believe it. I mean, isn't it hilarious when you think about it? If I'd a-been in a car wreck, at least it would've made sense. You'd better not charge a penny for your tests and everything. I don't care if insurance does cover it."

The nurse returned, spraying a jet of clear liquid from a needle.

Cal said, "Don't jab me with that. I can still bite, damn you! What is that? I have the right to know what you're doping me with."

Len rolled onto his abdomen and clamped the pillow tight around his head. He groaned and pressed his face in his sheets. Inject something lethal in his veins, and put him out of his misery. Toss his cadaver in the Montlake Canal. Let the birds pick him clean.

When Len woke up, someone had turned off the television, and his side of the room was dark. "Cal?" he called. The curtain shifted in the draft. Maybe he had already checked out.

A noise came from the hall: someone was leaning on the closed door, and her voice resonated through the wood: "That's all right, as long as you understand that you only have fifteen minutes left. Just a second, let me see if he's awake." The door opened, and the nurse said, "You have a visitor."

Len clicked on his light. "Okay," he said. "May I have an aspirin?"

"Do you have a headache?"

"Yes."

"Would you rather not see anyone right now?"

"No, that's fine."

"All right. I'll go get you something for your head."

She swung open the door, and Charis entered. She was pale in the fluorescent glow of the hall lights. "Hi," she said. She left the door open.

"Hello there. Have a seat."

"Thank you. I can't stay long."

"Want some candy? Sean and Julie left me some."

"No, thanks." Charis coughed and put a fist to her mouth.

Len said, "To tell you the truth, I'm surprised you came by. I thought I wouldn't ever see you again." She shrugged. He said, "You must have been pretty embarrassed."

"It isn't every day your date pees all over your skirt."

"I suppose not." Len opened and closed the top drawer of his dresser. "Hey, Charis, didn't you say something about me dying someday in an explosion? Remember, when we first met?"

"When we met? Oh, you mean at the party. No, no, no, that was just someone you reminded me of."

"Who was he? A lover?"

"He was my brother."

"I'm sorry."

"Yeah."

A nurse said from the hall, "Miss, I don't want to rush you out, but Dr. Amers is on the floor now, and he wanted to ask you a question or two in private. I'm sorry about that. I know you just got in."

"That's all right," said Charis. "Look, I'll be back in a minute, Len. Or if they won't let me back in tonight, I'll drop by tomorrow, maybe."

"Great." Though annoyed, Len disciplined himself to say nothing. "Take it easy."

"God!" Cal cried, and Charis started.

"Cal?" Len asked.

Charis scratched at a spot on her purse while he listened. She said, "He must be a joy to room with."

"He's all right," said Len. He pressed the call button for the nurse. "He usually doesn't talk in his sleep. He's pretty quiet most of the time."

Charis kissed him. "See you," she said.

Len laughed. "Good-bye."

"What are you laughing about? Have your lips turned ticklish?"

"No. It was nothing."

Charis smiled over her shoulder as she left and bumped into the nurse, who was entering. The nurse approached Len's bed. "Here's your aspirin," she said. "I'm sorry I forgot."

"No problem." Len swallowed the tablets with water from a paper cup.

"Well," said the nurse, leaning her bust on the bed rail, "she came back."

"What?"

"Your friend Charis. You said you'd never see her again."

"Yeah, I guess I did."

"Did you want anything else?"

"Oh, Cal was crying out a minute ago, and I thought maybe he needed some help, but when I tried to talk to him I realized he was unconscious."

"I'll check on him."

She went behind the curtain, and her squat form billowed the cloth where her shadow moved. She seemed to be making Cal's bed, tucking in the corners of his sheets, drawing her hand across his brow. Cal's light clicked out, and she reemerged.

"Good night, Len," she said.

"Good night, nurse."

"You still can't remember my name?"

He tugged on his lip and said, "I remember it was a Puritan name, something like Chastity or Prudence. What's so funny?"

"Nothing. You're wrong, though."

"It'll come to me. Hey, would you mind bringing me a TV schedule?"

"No, but I think you'd better get some sleep before those tests tomorrow. Sitting there for hours staring at lights and having wires hooked to your scalp can be exhausting. And that woman asks a lot of questions to keep your mind racing."

Len said, "Maybe she can save herself the bother and just electrocute me on the spot."

The nurse said, "That would be one way to keep you from running out on us."

She started for the door.

Len said, "Grace!"

"What?"

"Your name is Grace."

The nurse flashed her white teeth and laughed deeply. "No, but you're close," she said, stooping to pick up a get-well card that fluttered from his dresser. "Very close."

Resurrectionists

The light was purer than that of Port-au-Prince, Dale Rossin thought. Here in the mountains the air distilled light like white rum (he sipped his liqueur, viscous gold that clung to the inside of the glass), and although a breeze roiled dust from the road, the shadows were hard-edged like paper cutouts, and the atmosphere invisible, unlike the haze that filtered the sunlight and scumbled the arches, wooden balconies, and corrugated metal roofs in Port. Here you smelled pines and wet dust when it rained, not donkeys and sweat and rotting fruit and exhaust. In the mountains the nights were chilly, and at dawn when the sun glared on the cloud banks atop the ridges, the brightness hurt your eyes.

The shutters were half-open, and Rossin elbowed them out the rest of the way so he could feel the breeze. He dashed water and slivers of ice from his tumbler out the second-story window, nearly splashing some children playing down on the path (who yelled "Blanc!" and something else he did not understand), and pushed his chair back into the shade. Monsieur Fanfan, the landlord, had finally decided to clear Rossin's lunch dishes from the table out on the balcony, which overlooked the foothills and the plain where Port-au-Prince was etched alongside the sea. Fanfan clattered the dishes and stacked them on a tray. When he squinted at the room, Rossin beckoned, and the old man came to the door.

"I would like another glass of ice," said Rossin in French.

"Just ice? You are not drinking anything?"

"That's right. I just want to suck on some ice." He felt for his wallet in his back pocket.

Fanfan said something.

"What?" asked Rossin.

"I still have to charge you," said the landlord in English. "To make ice, I have to run a refrigerator. The electricity costs me money, you know."

"Of course," said Rossin.

A moment later Fanfan reappeared, carrying another tumbler on a green tray painted with the emblem of a European beer, a buxom Aryan girl carrying two frothing mugs of lager. The beer of Hitler youth. Fanfan was a mulatto with a Gaulish nose and sunken eyes; as he set the glass on the desk top, spotted with interlocking white rings from previous drinks, he glanced at Rossin's legs. He retrieved the other glass and departed. Rossin reached behind the leg of the desk, found his bottle of rum liqueur, and poured a shot over the ice.

Across the valley a bus ground down the mountain, blocked from view occasionally by a bend in the road, a primary-colored, thatched-roof house, or a cluster of pine and eucalyptus and almond trees. Rossin had caught a bus here on Friday—only yesterday: remember—from a provincial town down the road from the hospital where he had spent the last month. There had been no room inside the bus, so he had ridden on top in the luggage rack, with a pile of burlap sacks of charcoal, a goat, and eight other passengers, several of whom carried clucking chickens in their travel bags. One man kept watching Rossin, then finally climbed beside him to explain that they were passing the very crossroads where a cement truck had struck a bus ("Right outside the market-place, by the trestle there"); the accident had knocked the passengers from the roof of the bus into a gully where women were washing clothes.

Rossin had often seen half-naked women where the road crossed a river, lathering themselves with bars of soap or scrubbing blouses and trousers on rocks, and although the man's French was worse than Rossin's, the way he mimicked the women scrambling out of the way and snatching up pieces of laundry as they went was funny. But two passengers had died. "I heard that one of the corpses nearly washed out to sea," said the man, wiping his eyes. "It tumbled right down the wash onto the beach of a tourist hotel, and the waves carried it halfway down the beach, where a Belgian couple was learning to windsurf."

A fighting cock whose wattle and cockscomb had been removed thrust his masklike, sanguine head from the man's bag and glowered at Rossin. The man absently stuffed the bird back. "Were any chickens killed?" Rossin inquired. "Not to my knowledge," the man answered. "They can fly, you know. To get away from the wreck. Even my baby with his wings trimmed to fight can fly a little bit." He tried to kiss the rooster's head as it reemerged, but the bird pecked at his lips. After a moment he asked, "Are you a student?" Rossin answered, "No." The man nodded and said, "Most people your age who come here are students." "What?" asked Rossin, then grasped what the other had said. The bus lurched, and Rossin gripped the rail. "You seem very young," the man said. So had she. "I think they have a hard time estimating the age of Caucasians," she said, though even to Rossin she looked younger than twenty-four with her hair tied up in a scarf like a Haitian girl's, laughing and kicking the cold spray of the Pacific Ocean at him until he tackled and doused her.

Rossin stood and paced his room, feeling a disequilibrium until he realized he still wore his reading glasses, which distorted his peripheral vision, warping the ceiling fan, tearing pieces of wainscot from the walls and then replacing them as he turned. He removed his spectacles and set them on the desk beside a volume of the sermons of Meister Eckhart that he had carried from his home in south Florida. Rossin picked up the book and counted the pages he had read: twenty-one, or twenty-two if you counted the last half page. But he could not remember what he had read. An image remained of the crucified Son drawing the sympathy of the Father to mankind, perhaps only because of its vague ambience of unorthodoxy, but that was all.

He picked up a pen from the parallelogram of sunlight atop his desk. "As for Haiti, Jean," he wrote on a clean piece of paper, then sipped his rum, so flat and watery with melting ice that he reached under the desk for the bottle (he knocked it over, then righted it, the spilled liqueur soaking into the unfinished floor) and poured another shot into his glass. Rossin stared at the valley and saw that the sun sets and the shadows swallow the land even if it is your last weekend in a country and you are drunk:

> What do you want me to write? That this land obviated the longing for you or for the belief that brought me here? Perhaps that would be fitting, after my failure to comprehend what this place was for you and by extension for me (your silence being simply a void, a colorless uncharted spot in a sargasso sea, until I stepped from Dr. François Duvalier Airport and began shooing away the taxicab drivers and shoeshine boys). Nevertheless, it would be a lie. Neither your suffering nor the girl's nor whatever those corpses may have endured has deprived me of the absence of will that drew me like a vacuum to Hispaniola and keeps me, though dead inside, alive—

Rossin tore the page from his sketchpad, crumpled it, and threw it at a banana tree outside the window. The children hollered and scrambled for the paper. He decided that the girl Clarisse must have been watching him from the time he arrived at the hospital until a week later (he knew it had been her, now), when she came up behind him at a crowded spot on market day and pressed against his back and whispered, "Chéri!" Rossin had been haggling with an old woman for a few of the limes she had spread out on some rags at the edge of the road, and the old woman, fearful of losing her sale, abused the girl. The two bickered for a minute in rapid Creole, then the girl pushed her way back through the crowd before Rossin could get a good look at her.

The old woman shouted at him and snapped her fingers and even reduced her price a little in her anxiety that he might follow the girl, now just a headscarf bobbing away.

Rossin leaned on the desk and thought, Although I have been drinking steadily, I have not looked at that damn glass (the demon rum) in the last ten minutes; the ice and rum have been numbing my lips on their own. He bowed and moistened the paper with his brow, and he wondered if he should have gone ahead and sent the relief organization the photographs of the morgue. But of course the writer had refused to go in there, and it would have been senseless for a fund-raising pamphlet to publish pictures that would have repulsed the very people from whom it was trying to solicit donations: here is where we stack the ones who don't make it.

The room was off the hall where Rossin had been standing as he removed the filter from his camera. A surgeon peered around the corner and asked, "Who are you?" He was a short man, his head balding in an oval as if tonsured, and the skin seemed to have been peeled away from his pursed lips, pink along the mouth line. Rossin suddenly felt ridiculous: he was dressed like a doctor in loose green pants, tied with a drawstring, a green V-neck shirt, and a paper cap over his damp hair.

"My name is Dale Rossin. I'm a photographer." He touched the camera around his neck. "I'm taking photographs for a pamphlet about the hospital."

"Oh, yes. Your colleague interviewed me this morning. I am Dr. Devoix. Listen, would you lend me a hand here? Someone sent a body down to the morgue, and we have only one orderly to help. I could use some assistance shuffling things around."

Devoix led him around a corner to a bed on wheels covered with a sheet that suggested a human form: splayed feet, knees, thighs with cloth draped between them, the ridges of a pelvis, hands crossed on the breast, and a faceless head—an incompleted marble sculpture for a sepulcher. It was odd that some people preferred a grandiose monument, whereas when the choice had been Rossin's, he had selected a simple headstone without even a name engraved on it, so people would know that someone lay here and that they must not tread on this plot. A skinny teenager gripped the railing of the bed. "Open the door there, will you, uh, Mr. Rossin?" said Devoix. Rossin leaned across the stretcher and pushed the double doors open, and the doctor and boy shoved and pulled the bed through. Rossin followed them into the cool room, the only air-conditioned room in the hospital. Along one wall was a sink. Opposite were two stainless steel doors, one on top of the other. In the center of the floor stood a tile-covered table with a trough running around the top, presumably for performing autopsies; these, Devoix later told him, were a popular way of disposing of loved ones who had died in the hospital: the witch doctors could not cause a disemboweled and dissected body to rise again. Jean once left a magazine open to an article explaining how the voodoo doctors work their magic through a poison extracted from a blowfish, which left their victim comatose and almost without a heartbeat. Then the witch doctor could snatch the body (presumed dead, buried by the family) from the grave, administer drugs to revive it, and ritually rename the brain-damaged victim, who would serve as a slave, a zombie.

Rossin asked, "What did—he die of?"

The doctor shrugged. "I really couldn't say. This one was not one of my patients. Might have been anything." The question seemed to divert his attention, and he muttered, "I really should not do this anyway. I must prepare for surgery."

He yanked open one of the doors and dragged the top drawer halfway out. The drawer was piled with bodies in dirty white canvas bags. The bodies seemed frozen in a ferocious struggle to cast off their bags and free themselves.

"Too full," said Devoix. He leaned on the drawer while the orderly gave it a shove, and they managed to push it back and close the door. "Try the other one," he added in French.

Rossin helped open the lower drawer, which caught on its rollers. Two or three adult bodies lay under heaps of smaller bags like sacks of grain, the bodies of children. The orderly spoke in Creole. "Oui," said Devoix. He bent and picked up a sack in each hand and set them on the floor beside the stretcher, and the boy slid them aside with his foot. Then he too began unloading the sacks. Rossin snapped several pictures with his camera. Devoix looked up, sweating, then returned to his chore. Compositionally, the shots were better if you got low and caught the head of the corpse and the front legs and wheels of the stretcher, which balanced the black skin of the boy and the vertical movement of the drawer. A small russet poll slipped through the opening of a bag that the boy picked up, and Rossin remembered a child he had seen in the medicine ward the day before, hair tinted red from kwashiorkor, sipping milk from a tin cup, and he suppressed an urge to tear down the hall shoving people out of the way and check in the crib to see if the baby was still alive.

Finally, Devoix grabbed a brown-stained paper bag and flung it aside. A leaky package of discount meat on the refrigerator shelf. "What about this?" he asked Jean early on, before either of them knew. "I can barbecue these. You just sit down and rest." She looked at the tile countertop and said in a throaty voice, "No. I bought those lamb chops last week. They're too old. Throw them out." Rossin laughed: "Come on. They smell fine. Where's your sense of adventure? Besides, think of all the starving people in Haiti who'd give an arm and a leg for a lamb chop." He tore away the paper and unwrapped the cellophane and rinsed the dark blood from the meat. Threads of blood swirled in the sink and trailed down the drain. Jean left. Rossin laid the meat on a double layer of clean paper towels and poured her a glass of ice water. He brought it to her in the living room, but she was not lying on the couch. He found her in the bathroom, squatting before the toilet, sobbing dark strings of blood into the porcelain bowl. "Jean," Rossin said, "are you all right?" She wiped her mouth. "I'm sorry," she gasped. "It was the smell of the meat. Like the meat hanging in an outdoor market. And I started thinking—" She coughed, then settled back and became silent. Rossin knelt beside her and rubbed her back. "That place is tearing you apart," he whispered. "I know," she said, "I know." "Maybe you should give up—" Rossin said, then cut himself off as she glowered at him. And of course they learned that it had nothing to do with Haiti or the girl.

Devoix said, "Now, let us get this one in the drawer. Would you lend us a hand, Mr. Rossin?"

Rossin capped his lens. The doctor yanked the sheet away, as if performing a magic trick, making a body vanish before their eyes. This one too was in a canvas bag, with a pair of eggplant-colored feet and ankles extending from one end. The feet were broad and calloused; probably this man had been a mountain farmer who had never owned a pair of shoes in his life: you could imagine him treading unhurt on broken glass and bottle caps. He would wander across his field, misunderstanding the erosion of his soil; instead he would notice the rocks in his field growing larger every year and attribute this to the work of evil spirits.

Rossin stuck his hands under the man's shoulder blades. The warm flesh and boniness of the back and rib cage startled him. He said, "Should I just—" but the others grabbed the legs, and Devoix commanded, "All right, lift him," repeating his order in Creole. The head flopped back and clanged the rail of the bed. The boy jabbered; evidently he wanted to turn the body around and put it in feet first like the others, but he gave in, and they shoved it on top of the other bodies. Devoix and the boy piled the sacks on top, and last of all the doctor dropped the paper bag in the hollow of a child's corpse arranged in the fetal position. They pushed the drawer in and closed the stainless steel door.

As they walked from the morgue, Devoix tapped Rossin's arm and said, "The first day I came back after working in Montreal, I had five children die on me. Malnutrition-related. I no longer try to understand. I simply know this: all my patients end up here sooner or later, not in this room, but dead. Even Lazarus, after he was raised, did not live forever; he died again. So I ask myself, is this effort futile? And I have no answer."

Rossin nodded, scuffing at a black spot on the floor. "I guess I should go wash my hands."

"Good idea," said the doctor.

"Hey, would you mind if I observed this surgery of yours? A nurse is supposed to be showing me around, but I think she has forgotten me."

Devoix grimaced; perhaps it was intended as a smile. "Yes, that would be fine."

It was dark when he left the hospital, just as the valley darkened now, the lights of the city and the Route de Delmas blinking on. Rossin had walked to the house where he was staying, next door to one they had given the writer, who left at the beginning of the surgery when Rossin and several orderlies helped pin a raving patient to his bed until the sedatives went to work. The halfmoonlight shone bright enough to cast shadows in the ruts of the road and illuminate the ears and tail of a snarling cur that skulked past him. "Hey, white man, how's it going?" someone whispered as he trudged by. The air was still sweltering at nine o'clock, and Rossin's shirt was soaked with sweat from the slight physical effort of ascending the sloping path. A young man would fall into step with him and say, "Hey, blanc, what you look for? You want me show you round?" and Rossin would say a phrase in Creole that they said always worked in getting rid of beggars. And the man would continue, "I live in Miami one year till the immigration men get me. You from Miami? You know that town?" and Rossin would repeat the phrase. Finally, perhaps assuming that a blanc who knew Creole was no easy sucker, the man would tire and slow his pace and fall back.

The doors and windows of the houses were open, and

Rossin descried the dark shapes of people in the pale glow of kerosene tin can lamps, and heard the storytelling in a language that sounded like rosewood sticks clattering down a stairway, and smelled the charcoal fires and rice and beans cooking. A chicken clucked and fluttered across his path. Cinema would be the medium to catch this place: the light, the slow, profound motions; and of course they say that film does not lie, it simply observes—the bodies, for example, though as a photographer he knew that an infinite number of lies were committed in the act of preserving light and dark on film.

He reached the house where he was staying, one of two on this side of town with a metal roof (the other the writer occupied), small, white, removed from the road and sitting beside a neglected garden plot. He decided to continue walking uphill, to a rise where the houses thinned out. A hundred yards later he met the girl coming down the path.

"Bon soir, chéri," she said.

"Bon soir."

"You want me, blanc? One dollar," she said in English.

"No, thanks. I'm not interested."

She turned and followed Rossin up the hill. "Yes, I see you interest, chéri."

He used the Creole phrase, "I have no money for you today," but she only laughed. "Blanc no got money? What happen, you get rob?"

Rossin ignored her.

She walked closer, brushing his arm. "What is wrong? You no like black girl?"

Rossin laughed.

"No, that's not it."

"You got girl at home in America?"

"No. Not anymore."

"You got me, chéri." She reached for his hand, but Rossin lifted his arm and looked at his watch. The path amid the cacti beyond the outskirts of town was steeper and rockier, and Rossin stumbled. He stopped and rested his hands on his hips and tried to ignore her breathing beside him and her form in the corner of his eye. She seemed less winded than he. Lamps flickered in the windows and on the porches of the houses that lined the crooked lanes and alleys of town, and in the distance the hospital's even electric lights glowed through the screened windows. The girl moved closer. She was slender, with broad cheekbones, and although she was missing a cuspid she was beautiful. Her dress was open in front, revealing the smudged line of her breasts and a glimpse of a nipple. One often saw women in front of their shacks pounding corn in a hollowed-out stump, their dresses unbuttoned and their pectorals working and their dugs flapping about on their rib cages, until one ceased to notice, but this woman was young and her breasts were smooth and attractive. The girl's dress seemed clean and store-bought, and this made Rossin feel better.

"I don't think so," he said.

She patted his right pants pocket. "You got money, blanc. I see the place." He took a deep breath, stuffed his hand in his pocket, and clutched the wad of waxy five-gourde notes, perhaps twenty of them, each worth a dollar.

She said, "How long you here in Haiti?" She gathered her skirt and pulled it tight around her thighs and hips.

"I'm not sure how long I'll stay. I've been here a couple of weeks."

"Then you go home—after you leave?"

"No, I'll go somewhere else. Maybe California."

"You need a Haitian girl."

"No, I don't."

Rossin turned and walked back down the hill. Where the path broadened into a road he walked on the opposite side from his house. Here the path was smoother, and he thought, *She was going in this direction in the first place; even if she was to come down the hill she would not be following you;*

and then, hearing her footsteps in the dust behind him: you could just hand her the money and she will be as happy, although maybe she genuinely desires to sleep with you, and one must in any case refuse flat out to give money to beggars, because the word gets out.

Jean never gave away money. On their trip to San Francisco, they had bought cracked crab and sourdough bread at Fisherman's Wharf and then driven to Golden Gate Park, where Rossin spread out a blanket on the grass, ready for the two of them to relax and enjoy the afternoon, when a bum approached them. His head was wrapped in dirty gauze. One arm hung in a sling, and his hands were bandaged. "Got any spare change?" he asked, and Rossin, thinking to get rid of him quickly (today, of all days), dug in his pockets. However, Jean answered, "No, but we'll share our lunch with you." "I can't eat crab," the bum said, "I couldn't get it out of the shell." He raised his hands in their mitts of bandages. "Sit down and join us," said Jean. The old man looked at Rossin, who nodded. He knelt beside them. Jean broke the crab apart, piece by piece, and fed the old man, putting the white, red-tinged meat on his tongue. The bum's face reddened and wrinkled up, and he began blubbering as he chewed the crab and bread openmouthed. When he finished eating, he told them he had fallen off a train, and a sheriff's deputy found him unconscious in a ditch and took him to a hospital in Oakland. "God, lady," he concluded, "you're the first person who has done anything good for me since I hit the streets twelve years ago." After the man left, Rossin teased, "Why did you do that, little girl?" but she refused to answer. Her fingertips and painted nails touched those sticky wine-stinking lips. They did not hold hands as they returned to the car.

Rossin's shoe kicked up a rock. One five-gourde note. He crossed the road to his house and passed through the wooden gate in the chalky cactus fence, leaving it creaking on its hinges. He walked, his shoes crackling, along the gravel path to the porch, fished for his key, hearing the hinges squeak behind him, and unlocked the sets of blue double doors to the mud-and-wattle hut. Let out the daytime heat and the odors of mouse droppings, grease, and this morning's fried eggs. Specks of red and blue swirled in the darkness, and the moon cast his shadow on the whitewashed wall. Rossin did not look back. The girl was in the yard, he guessed, but he hoped she would stand at the other side of the house (if she insisted on following him), where no passerby could spot her. He turned around. She was leaning against a twisted old oak that he had never noticed before; even from the porch she was only a smudge against the bark. "No money," he said in Creole to make sure she understood, "go away," but then he hesitated for a moment, and she came toward the house. He remembered Jean in bed with only a sheet over her, lying on her side while she traced an arabesque on his back.

Rossin stepped inside to open the other doors and the shutters. The woman came to the threshold, the light through her skirt silhouetting her legs. He struck a match, which flared so that his field of vision was reduced to a small globe around him, and lifted the sooty chimney of the lamp, but as the flame approached his fingers he shook it out: I do not want to draw the neighborhood children like little moths to stare into the white man's house at night. She waited with her hand on the door, and Rossin feigned surprise at still finding her there, "Yes?" She entered the room, evidently believing she had his permission, and came to him and put her arms around his neck. He held her shoulders. They were thin and bony, and he shuddered. But her hands caressed his back. Her hair was braided in ridges along her scalp. She pressed her belly against him and kissed his lips, and Rossin stumbled a little as he pulled her against himself. "Listen—" he said and tried to disengage himself, but she clung to him. Her dress slipped from one shoulder. She kissed him again. "Oui, chéri," she said. Her lips tasted like cloves.

"No. I'm sorry."

"One dollar. I see you like me."

"One dollar."

"I know you got lots of money."

Rossin thrust her away, and she tripped and fell to the concrete floor. One of her shoes came off, and she crawled over and reached for it under the table and pulled it on.

"I'm sorry. I didn't mean to knock you over." Rossin took her arm and helped her up, then wedged his hand in his pocket and peeled a five-gourde note from his wad of bills. "Here." The girl snatched the bill, folded it, and tucked it into a pocket on the front of her dress. "There's your money, okay?" he said. "Now listen, I want to talk to you for a moment."

The girl pulled her dress up on her shoulder and crossed her arms.

"Do you want to sit?" Rossin moved a wooden chair out from the table by the wall.

"No."

"What's your name?"

She moved toward the back door, but he grabbed her wrist. She writhed and tried to free herself in the pale, distorted reflection off the corrugated aluminum shower stall outside the open door. "Wait, come here." Rossin dragged her over and sat her down at the table. "I go now," she said, and put her hand on the pocket over her breast. "Okay, just a minute," said Rossin. "I'm not going to take your money."

She relaxed, and he let go of her arm and sat in a chair opposite her. "What's your name?"

"Clarisse."

Rossin was unsure what else he wanted to ask her. "Do you live here in town?"

"Why you ask?"

"I'm just curious about you."

"Nearby."

"You got any children?"

The girl slumped slightly. "Two children, but one die last Easter. The baby sick now too."

"Are you married?" He regretted the question at once.

Clarisse glared at him, he felt, although even with his eyes adjusted to the dark he could not make out her expression. "I no got man. Them Tontons Macoutes—you know them? They—" She waved her fist, and for a moment he thought she would strike him; it would have been a good punch too: him leaning forward, elbows on his knees, jaw exposed. But she lowered her hand and touched his knee. "This neighbor let his donkey eat in our field, you know. My man complain, so the neighbor tie the donkey on rope. But the rope too long, and the donkey still eat corn. So my man cut the rope with machete and tie it short. But this man got friend in Tontons Macoutes, and they come at night and"—pah! she smacked her palm—"they beat him, you know, and they hack him with machete and leave him dead. I sold the field to get money to bury him."

She made a low noise in her throat. Rossin handed her his handkerchief, and she blew her nose and stuffed it in her pocket with the money.

"I'm sorry," said Rossin.

"Why you ask all this?"

He shrugged and then, afraid she discerned only a vague stirring in the dark, said, "I don't know."

A cricket buzzed through the louvered window and glanced off a poster on the wall. Then it flew at the ceiling, struck the metal with a ping, and dropped to Rossin's lap. He flicked the cricket away, and Clarisse laughed.

"You scare of insect?"

"Only when they attack me like that."

She sprang from her chair. "Wait," said Rossin, vexed. She stood with a hand on the doorpost. He started to dig in his pocket, then remembered some money he had dropped behind the table that morning, and he leaned over with one hand on the cool concrete and found it. Several coins slipped through his fingers and jingled across the floor through the back door. From the size of the bills he guessed they were more five-gourde notes. Rossin stood and found her hand in the dark, the roughened fingers, and gave her the money. Clarisse clenched the bills, catching the tip of his thumb, and stared at him. He bent and kissed her cheek, and her hoarse breath warmed his ear. "For the baby," he said, then insisted, though she had not refused, "take it." Clarisse crumpled the bills and pocketed them. She darted out the door. Rossin wondered if she would search the grass for the coins that had rolled out, but to his vague disappointment she trotted around the shower stall and disappeared. He sat on the foot of the bed, choking back a sob, and sorted in the trash basket for the cricket that rustled around among scraps of paper.

"Haiti Chérie": this was the one thing Jean had refused to share with him. Eight months after their wedding, the story broke about the Haitian woman accused of murdering her baby amid (a neighbor who did not wish to be quoted had whispered) chanting and drums and bleating, unearthly voices. A police sergeant speculated that the ritual had involved a number of objects possibly connected to voodoo that were found in her apartment: bottles of noisome potions, said a detective who had uncapped and sniffed each one; a straw man in which the careful observer could detect pinpricks; pieces of bone and feathers; a small cloth bag of bread pinned over the doorway. Yet Jean scoffed at the quotes and the article and Rossin's photograph of daylight filtering through the wire mesh of the slum apartment's window and illuminating the crib.

"Did we get the story wrong? Tell me," Rossin begged her. "That's the kind of thing a newspaper needs to know."

Jean said only, "You wouldn't understand without going there."

He said, "I tried to go there, and you were the one who didn't want to return. Don't blame me if the paper doesn't share your cultural sensitivity."

Jean frowned at him but remained silent. Of course Rossin was right—he had suggested they go to Haiti on their honeymoon, sure the idea would please her, but she was aghast, "Don't be silly. I don't want to go back there now, with you. I can just imagine it: lying awake at the Club Med in sweaty sheets, listening to the drums pounding in the hills, or drinking cocktails as we watch one of those fake ceremonies they stage for whites while a man tears out a chicken's entrails with his teeth."

Instead they flew to San Francisco, rented a car, and drove up Highway 101, along the Pacific Coast, where the cliffs and fog and forests of firs and hemlocks and madronas were as unlike the hot, treeless, tropical vistas of Hispaniola as anything one can find on any coastline. But Jean could not dismiss Haiti's indwelling. She had gone a Christian and returned two years later an agnostic, and Rossin, who had relinquished his faith at twelve without a second thought, following his mother's example when his parents divorced, found her grief and torment difficult to apprehend. And he was only further confused when he returned home from work the last day Jean saw the Haitian woman and found his wife curled up in a ball beside the couch, arms around her knees, rocking and singing "Haiti Chérie" to herself. He was frightened that she took it so hard, and he told her he was sorry. But instead she spoke about a voodoo priest that she had met one day while visiting a town called Hinche, an old man with streaks of gray whiskers on his cheeks. Even after the doctor assured them there was nothing psychosomatic about Jean's illness, Rossin found this hard to believe.

Rossin left the hospital a week after he finished his assignment. Devoix offered him a ride to a nearby town where he had business. "It's only thirty-five kilometers in your direction, but you hit the worst of the road in my Land Rover instead of a bus." Rossin accepted.

As they started out of town, Devoix asked, "Have you ever tasted clairin?"

"Clairin?"

"You would remember if you had. It is the rum the peasants drink."

Rossin had not.

"I will have to buy you a shot. You cannot leave Haiti without drinking clairin. Forget this Barbancourt stuff you buy in the nice shops. This is real bathtub rum."

The doctor pulled his Land Rover to the side of the dirt road along a row of shops and restaurants painted pink, yellow, blue, and white. "Come with me," he said. He stepped out and jumped over a concrete ditch, about two feet deep, flowing with water and strands of moss, and transversed by occasional planks. A swirl of dust overtook the vehicle, obscuring the doctor, as Rossin got out. Devoix led him down the boardwalk to a dirty pink building whose façade was intricately carved with flowers and star and moon shapes and laughing faces, before which a group of men in straw hats stood drinking beer. He began dickering with an old woman sitting at a card table covered with bottles.

Next door a crowd had gathered around a guitarist who sat on the boardwalk with his legs crossed like a sitar player's, one ankle over the other knee. The strings of his instrument were tautened with pieces of twisted paper, and as he crooned the man thrummed as if his guitar was a percussion instrument. Above him on the blue-and-yellow wall, linking the two fields of color, the word BANK was lettered vertically, the A partially obscured by a poster someone had pasted up, of Pope John Paul II and President-for-Life Jean-Claude Duvalier, who smirked like a schoolboy (nicknamed Fatty, no doubt) making naughty gestures out of view of the camera.

(Jean Paul. Jean-Claude. How different the name looked in French from the familiar JEAN inscribed on the leather of the

English-style saddle her parents had given her as a girl, the one thing of her possessions that he had returned to them.) The expression on the president's face seemed to indicate that, *en balance,* he was delighted with the Holy Father's visit, despite the criticism the pope had leveled against the Duvalier regime, perhaps even while smelling the garbage in the air as he spoke (though American newspapers had reported that Duvalier had trucked his piles of trash and hordes of poor people from the streets of Port-au-Prince in honor of the pope's upcoming visit). After all, except for the phrase "Things must change!" John Paul had spoken in French, a language foreign to ninety percent of the Haitian population, and now the president of the republic had pictures of himself and the bishop of Rome to paste on walls throughout the country, and the ubiquitous image of the two men together must have deeply impressed the peasants.

"I want to see that country. My wife said from her time working there that the Haitians are a profoundly visual people," Rossin had told his managing editor as an afterthought, though the man needed no persuading and was relieved to grant an unpaid leave to his moping, unproductive photographer. The crowd's attention strayed to Rossin as he photographed them, and they began begging in Creole, "Take my photo! One dollar!" ruining the shots with their outstretched hands. He returned to the doctor, who seemed to have bargained the clairin seller down to a reasonable price.

"Bon soir, blanc," said one of the beer drinkers. "Give me one dollar"—the phrase everyone seemed to know. Rossin ignored the man.

Devoix turned to his companion. "I bought you a dime's worth," he said, grinning. "It might be too much."

The clairin vendor said in Creole, "It will make you drunk." She rubbed her hands together, delighted at the prospect. Devoix added, "You don't need to drink all of it. I will have some."

The vendor uncorked a corncob stopper from a rum bottle

whose label had been peeled away, then poured the clear liquid through a funnel into the spotty beer bottle until it was two-thirds full. She was a tiny woman, milky brown in complexion and freckled with moles. She thrust the bottle at Rossin, and the beer drinkers moved closer. A crowd gathered behind them and out in the road.

"Drink quickly," said Devoix.

Rossin took a deep breath. Then he raised the bottle and chugged the clairin, scalding his throat with the drink, coarser than any rum he had ever drunk: the clear rectified liquor frothed in the bottle before his nose and lips. He thought, Sucking like a zoo ape on its mother's teat. The people he glimpsed in the slivers of peripheral vision between the bottle and his cheeks shouted and nudged one another. Sweat poured from his face. Rossin finished the bottle and handed it to the vendor, his eyes weeping. He whooped. The crowd applauded and cheered.

"It's strong," he gasped in French.

"Yes, very strong," said the beaming old woman.

Devoix slapped him on the shoulder. "I cannot believe you have drunk all of this. I would have drunk some of it for you."

Rossin wiped his mouth. "John Wayne would never have forgiven me."

"Good?" asked the woman in English. "Good?"

"Yes, good. Outstanding. Burned the lining out of my stomach. Merci, madame."

"Oui, oui. Merci, monsieur."

"I am getting myself a soft drink," said Devoix. "Do you want one?"

"Thanks, that sounds great. A cola."

Rossin climbed into the Land Rover. The clairin churned in his stomach, but his head was still oblivious to the rush of alcohol that was about to suffuse his blood vessels. He would probably die in the tropical heat. At least he had a physician with him. He closed his eyes.

Rossin felt a shadow on his face, and thinking it was another beggar, he kept his eyes closed. Go ahead: slit the white man's throat and take his money, he's too drunk to resist. Then he heard the voice ("Hey, chéri, you go now?"), and his skin prickled. Clarisse leaned in the window, and her beautiful face with its broad cheekbones and flared nostrils was close. Her eyes were yellowed and bloodshot, and sweat beaded her upper lip and her sternum between her breasts. She was wearing a new black dress and red earrings. A man in a straw hat stood back on the road, grinning at them.

Rossin looked at the dark, low doorway of the shop into which the doctor had disappeared. "Yes. I am going."

"You like clairin? I see you drink."

"Yes. It was good."

"How you feel? You drink too much?"

"No. I feel fine."

"Chéri, my baby sick bad. You got money for him? He need hospital, and I no got money."

"I no got money either, okay? I gave you money the other day."

The doctor emerged from the shop with an orange and a brown bottle, pausing to nod—almost bow—to the vendor, like an acolyte passing before the altar.

"Yes, but he sick bad, and I spend all the money already. Please."

Devoix lumbered into the vehicle and handed Rossin the bottle of cola. The striated glass was grimy and wet, and the cold bottle shocked Rossin's hand. He touched it to his brow.

"How are you?" Devoix asked.

"A bit light-headed is all." He drew some money from his pocket. "What do I owe you?"

Devoix swallowed and waved the money away. "My treat."

"Hey, give me this money," said Clarisse. "Please."

Rossin tucked the money away. "What do you do about these people?" he asked Devoix.

The doctor swigged his soda. "Ignore her. We have beggars everywhere in Haiti, and they are worse in this town because of all the kindhearted doctors and nurses who work here for a few months and give everything away before they return home."

Clarisse protested in Creole, "I'm hungry," rubbing her belly, perhaps pregnant, the full flesh surrounding the indentation of a navel against the fabric of her dress, a view blocked now and then by her breasts as she leaned against and pulled back from the car door.

"I know," said Devoix.

He clamped the orange soda between his knees and worked the stick shift into reverse. Clarisse chattered to him in Creole, running along with them as they backed out. The Land Rover paused, and Devoix said something to her as he fought the shift into first gear. He gestured, nearly swatting Rossin's ear, and they lurched forward. "Please, chéri!" Clarisse pleaded. She grabbed at Rossin's neck but hooked her thumbnail in his collar buttonhole, gouging his skin. He shoved her hand away, but she clutched his shirt sleeve. The people on the boardwalk gawked and pointed in astonishment and shouted to each other. The vehicle took off and jerked the woman loose, and they sped down the road. Sweat stung Rossin's neck.

Devoix glanced at him. "You're bleeding."

Rossin pulled a handkerchief from his hip pocket and dabbed at his neck.

"I'm sorry about that," said Devoix. "She told me her baby is sick. She is very desperate."

"Oh." Rossin's handkerchief was blood-spotted, recalling an Edvard Munch painting of a blood-flecked child in a woman's arms. He ventured, "What did you say to her?"

"I told her to see me at the hospital tomorrow." The road was momentarily smooth as they crossed a bridge over an irrigation canal. Rice paddies stretched from the road to the rusty, gully-riddled mountains across the valley, and palm trees flickered past. "Why did she call you chéri?" the doctor asked.

"I don't know."

Devoix rolled his window down and adjusted the side mirror. He said, "How are you feeling after all of this clairin?"

"Not bad. I've got a slight headache."

"I won't be of any assistance to you if you die. I am afraid I didn't bring any leeches with me."

A van broke down on the road below the hotel. The floodlight on the balcony illuminated a patch of hillside and the side of the van, brightly painted, its panel framed by two snakes raised on staffs (Rossin laughed aloud when he noticed them) and an arabesque of blue, red, and yellow; the panel depicted a black Christ kneeling on a lawn beside a stream and sweating bright rubies of blood. Passengers grumbled and milled about on the road, and two women eventually bawled out the driver, then balanced their baskets atop their heads and set off up the hill. A white couple climbed out of the van and groaned and stretched. The woman was freckled, and she sulked prettily. Rossin pressed his fingers hard against his eyeballs.

"At least it's cooler here," the woman said.

The man rubbed her arms. "I know. How long do you think it will take them?"

The driver was working under the van, and the woman tapped his leg with her foot. "How long will it be?" she said. The reply was muffled. "Time," she said. "How much time will it take?"

The driver crawled out from under the vehicle and wiped his hands on a rag. "Comment?"

"Time. How long will it be?" She touched her wrist.

The driver consulted his watch and showed it to her. "Li uit è edemi, madame."

"He doesn't understand you," said the husband. "I think that was the time. Excuse me, but is there a hotel in this town? You know, sleep?" He folded his hands against his cheek. "Hotel for blancs?"

The woman said, "We need a translator."

That was the whole problem. Jean was the only person fluent enough in Creole to translate for the woman, and of course she had volunteered, almost spitefully, Rossin thought, after she saw the admittedly stupid blunders in the article. ("Abrams said that despite the presence of a Spanish-speaking officer, LaSalle seemed baffled by the arrest. One officer who requested anonymity was more blunt. 'She had no idea what was going on,' he said. 'I don't even think she can speak.'")

But after the verdict Rossin came home, having taken a photograph of a deputy escorting the handcuffed woman from the courthouse, and found Jean on the floor. He sat beside her and put his arms around her. "I'm sorry she lost," he lied. Jean said, "Don't you know—" then cut herself off. Instead she told him about a conversation she had had one blazing dusty day: "The priest said it isn't like a pious moral guideline for living. You become one with what you fear and worship. But not like her." "No," said Rossin. Jean added, "She'll be electrocuted. And maybe she deserves it. She said a spirit possessed her, compelled her to do it. Maybe she is insane, but it's not like these people murder their children any more than we would." And then those words: "But you wouldn't understand, would you?" "No," Rossin acceded, "maybe not."

The man rubbed his nose and said, "There's no point in going on at this hour. We can find a hotel in a town this size. What's that up there? Is that a blanc up on the balcony?" Hollering: "Pardon me, do you speak English?"

Rossin stood up unsteadily and carried the chair and his glass and bottle back to his room (he drank openly now, muttering to himself, much to Fanfan's displeasure). It was still overheated in the thick-walled building, but Rossin hated the electric lightbulb hanging from the ceiling, so he lit a kerosene lamp on the bedstand, despite the heat it put out. He collapsed on the bed and kicked off his shoes. Several coins slipped from his pocket and clinked on the floor. Sunday was only an hour or so away, and then one more day: he had enough left to pay Fanfan and perhaps buy some breadfruit in the marketplace, and of course he needed to save the fare for a minivan down to the airport.

Christ. Devoix had been aghast. "You don't have to pay me," he said. Rossin flushed now, as then: "No, you see, in case a woman comes in with a sick child and can't afford the hospital—or if she doesn't come, there are others who might need it, in the tubercular ward, for instance." Devoix nodded and stuffed the money in the glove box and stared at the steering wheel as he said good-bye. They looked like skeletons in the tubercular ward. So did she. She said, "Thanks, but I don't think I could get it down." Her weight had dwindled to seventy-five pounds, and she was balding, her lips chapped and crusted. "How about water?" Dale suggested. Jean ignored him. "Will you get me a minister?" she said. Rossin asked, "A minister?" "Yes," Jean insisted. "And not that goddamn Unitarian chaplain. Someone who believes. That minister at First Presbyterian—what's his name? I should remember, I visited a couple of times when you were working Sundays." But when the tanned minister arrived, dressed in sweats, all he could do was frown at her body and mumble, "I'm so sorry it took me this long to get here." Rossin said, "Aren't there any last rites you can perform?" "Not in the Presbyterian church," the minister said. "But we can pray. Will you pray with me?" And Rossin in agony said, "You pray. That's what I brought you here for." He walked from the room.

Now, as Rossin lay on the bed, a mosquito bit his foot. Smear the insect bloody. He fumbled an insect coil from a box on the bedstand and tried to impale it on a spike in the ashtray, where it was supposed to burn (a martyr, a heretic), but the coil snapped. He flung the pieces at the wall. They shattered and scattered across the floor. On his second try, he managed to place another coil and light it, and the smoke filled his nostrils, a soothing aroma, staying my wrath. He tasted coffee and rum on his lips.

Somebody shuffled about and thumped luggage out on the balcony. "What about that room on the end?"

"That one—a young man is staying there, sir."

"Probably the one you saw, Ray."

"Probably. I'll bet he's a Frenchman. The French are so damned haughty. He wouldn't speak to us."

"Yes, I am certain he is French. They are all that way."

"I see he had fish for dinner."

"Oh, I will clean that up, madame. He ate very late."

"Well, I guess this will have to do for the night."

"Hey, is there a pool here?"

"I am sorry, sir, but my pool is temporarily closed for repair. The Frenchman in the end room likes to swim in the river just up the road. Anyway, I am sure you will be most comfortable."

"Thanks. I think we'll manage."

"God, I wonder why we left the club. Listen—wait a second. Can we drink the water here, or will that kill us?"

"Oh, no, madame. The water is very clean. I get it from a spring."

Rossin kicked his door shut. Death by water. Idiot. Below his window people chattered in Creole (the sound of rosewood sticks), and their voices grew indistinct as they descended the path where the children had been playing and headed down the road. A whiff of cigarette smoke. Drums pounded in the hills, and faint voices sang songs that resounded with a profound yearning for Africa, a union, they said, the other side of death that would forever separate them from this island; they sang believing that death comes to the quick as well as the walking dead. What day was this? Jesus, it couldn't be. A voodoo festival, followed by a Roman Catholic holiday tomorrow, linked like Siamese twins: Day of the Dead, All Saints' Day. Dogs throughout the valley barked like scattered foghorns.

Rossin stripped to his shorts and lay back on the bed. Knowing he would not sleep, he did not bother to extinguish the lamp. What was the verse that writer chose as a title? Would that I had died instead of thee. Or that death had swallowed us both. Rossin wished he could study his face without going down the hall to the bathroom to look in the mirror. No matter how desperate the eyes, it always soothed you to see your smooth cheeks and forehead, face youthful, still uncorrupted, stubbled with the evening blue of whiskers.

Then Dale Rossin closed his eyes and fitfully recalled the morgue and the drawer pulled out, catching on its rollers, and in his mind he tried to erase the bodies or transfer them to stone tombs of the sort you saw right after the police checkpoint on the road into Hinche: painted bright colors and decorated with tin flowers, but an individual sepulcher for each corpse, even the sacks of grain or meat. The resurrection, the resurrection, the resurrection would be a comfort, if it was a spiritual one that did not require matter, atoms and molecules, this darksome house, to rise again. But instead he saw a body, still enshrouded in its bag, standing on its roughened feet on the tile floor, struggling like Lazarus to free itself. By this time it will stink, for he had been dead four days. Unbind him, and let him go. Rossin opened his eyes and stared at a water stain on the ceiling, terrified.

Shooting

We always drank after work on Thursdays. For a while it died out when the fog and rain cleared up and the weather got better and some people headed off to golf, but then on a slow, overcast afternoon someone said, "Let's go grab a beer." I said, "What the hell. I can't stay long, though"—I had plans for dinner. But they decided to go not to a tavern where you could chug a quick pitcher, but to the inn on the river with the expensive drinks in which the bartender plopped bright sweet pickled vegetables and plastic mermaids that clung to the side of your glass. The day was muggy. The sky was clearing in the west, and we sat out on the deck in the hot sunshine while the sun descended in its steep downward arc and the river glowed brighter and brighter on either side of a small island where the stream parted. I wanted something with ice in it, gin and tonic. Then I remembered the line from the movie, and I said in an English accent like the old colonel out by the pool in Jakarta, "Americans drink gin and tonic with ice. We're not Americans," and everybody laughed. "You'd better make his a double," said a copy editor (stifling a belch) who had been sitting close enough to hear what the woman had told me that afternoon—although everyone in the newsroom was looking by the time she broke down and cried.

The blonde waitress with a fine embroidery of capillaries on one cheek brought us our drinks. A man on a jet boat kept racing down the river past the deck, turning around under the bridge and speeding back upstream, leaving a rooster tail spraying behind him. The engine whined infuriatingly. The man wore a red helmet. I thought, A red skullcap, and winced. I muttered, "Christ." The copy editor was watching me. He said, "Don't worry. That happens to everyone." The man in the jet boat kept glancing up at us, perhaps thinking we found him a daredevil. We could not converse. When he sped by the fourth time, I snatched up a saltshaker and flung it at him and quickly leaned back in my chair, looking in the other direction. Everyone laughed. Someone was saying, "Did he throw it? Did he really throw it?" "You can see it in the water right there. That white spot." I ignored them. The waitress came by and I smiled at her. The jet boat came whining back. A group of people from our table got up and stood by the rail and covered their ears or gave him the thumbs-down sign. Even through his visor he looked angry and embarrassed. I stayed at the table. The boat did not return downriver. "Victory," said the copy editor, sitting down in his chair. I made a joke, and we laughed until our eyes watered. I forget what I said.

"Don't tell his friend," someone said, perhaps later. "Can you imagine your own girlfriend busting you for reckless mischief: hurling a projectile at a boat driver?"

Then I was alone in my apartment with a discounted bottle of Muirhead's scotch whisky. I undid my tie and removed it. I kept my mind from straying and thought instead about the liquor. I remember pacing and throwing a chair and watching it tumble and bounce once and knock something over. The scotch was not bad when you considered what you paid for it. I toyed with the notion of pouring whatever was left down the drain when I was finished for the evening, but it was a shame to think of dumping it, even if Muirhead's is not the best you can buy. (Whoever heard of reporters drinking the best? You make less than schoolteachers.) You might as well set money on fire. The chair was on its side. I righted it.

I looked at the clock and thought, Damn, I'm late for work. The doorbell rang again. I was sprawled across the bed with the *Wall Street Journal* draped across my chest, wearing only my underwear, and I knew only she would keep ringing the bell like that. My heart was pounding, and I tried hard to think why she would come by. I had scribbled comments on an article in the *Journal,* but now my felt-pen scrawl made no sense, and I could pick only an occasional phrase out of the tangled words zigzagging across the page, smeared where I had spilled scotch. I pulled on a pair of gym shorts and brushed my teeth and gargled with mouthwash while the bell kept ringing. I dashed over and answered the door—she was starting down the stairs. She wore a blue jacket, the color of her uniform; her dark hair always looked pretty against the navy blue.

"Don't leave yet," I said.

"Hi. There you are. Were you asleep?"

"No. I was in the bathroom."

"Oh, I'm sorry to disturb you. Did you forget we were going to have dinner tonight?"

"Of course not. I just took a nap when I got home, and I overslept. I woke up just before you got here."

The sun was setting, and she stood out in front in the evening air, looking at me. I grinned. Long rays of sun suffused the air, and I remembered Homer, fingertips of rose. Fingertips of blood stroking the child's blood-soaked hair.

"I can come back another night."

"No, it'll only take me a second to get dressed. What time is it?"

"Eight-thirty."

"I'm really sorry. Come on in."

She entered my apartment. "Sorry about the mess," I said. Papers and books, the overflow of my limited shelf space, were scattered across the floor, and the half-empty bottle lay beside the couch. A potted fern was kicked over in the corner, spilling its dry, white-speckled dirt on the carpet. She set it upright.

"How did this happen?"

"I don't know. I must have kicked it over on my way to work this morning."

I kissed her and went into my room to dress, calling through the door, "So how was your day?"

"Fine," she said, right next to me, and I saw she was watching me dress. I laughed.

"Sexy," she said.

I grinned at her, stumbled pulling on my jeans, and put my hand on her shoulder for balance. She kissed my knuckles. At the restaurant I drank water with my dinner. She had a beer, but I was not even tempted. She looked pretty the way she sipped, bobbing her head, lowering her upper lip to the foam. I said, "Did I tell you about the kid and that gun today?" "Yes. And it was on the scanner." I unfolded my napkin and said, "I don't know if you heard the kid died this afternoon, after the paper was out. I don't know why the hell people with children keep loaded guns in the house. By the time I got there I thought they would have taken him away, but he was still there on the stretcher at the foot of the ambulance, wearing diapers. His blond hair was plastered against his scalp, and his mother was standing there in her bathrobe, crying. After the paper came out and she read what I wrote, she came in and screamed at me. She thought I made it sound like it was her fault." She looked at me. I said, "I told you that already."

"Yes, when you were dressing."

"You distracted me, staring at me like that. How do you expect me to remember?"

She smiled.

I said, "What did you do today?"

"I already told you."

"I was kidding." I was sober now. "You busted that crank lab up on Elk River Drive."

"Very good."

"You could have busted some ruffians at the inn after work today. That would be a feather in your cap. The whole *Dispatch* newsroom."

"I hope you didn't drive afterward."

"Don't leap to assumptions. I didn't really get plastered till I got home. That's why I took a nap: to sleep it off."

"Good." She watched a fat man scurry out of the kitchen,

carrying a bucket of croutons to the salad bar. She was never judgmental. I liked that.

I asked, "What was the lab worth? You told me that. Twenty-five thousand dollars."

"Right."

"And one of the officers bit some guy who tried to escape?"

She laughed. "No, that was Corporal Boone."

"Boone?"

"He's a dog."

She touched my hand. The waitress brought our orders of steak and scallops and clattered the platters on the table. We began eating.

"Why did that woman think you were blaming her?"

"Oh, in my story I wrote, 'Deputies are investigating the incident.' The mother thought that sounded like she and her husband were suspects in a murder. Maybe she didn't like the small amount of description I put in it, about the kid in his diapers. She said I was cold-blooded. I didn't say anything. I told her I was sorry. When she left I went into the bathroom and locked the door of the stall and sat there. I was terribly empty. I wanted to get drunk."

She nodded, looking at her plate.

"Child abuse is the worst for me."

"I don't think that was a case of abuse."

"I know. I was just commenting."

I noticed the way she drank. She looked pretty, suds clinging to her upper lip. She wiped her mouth with her napkin.

"What are you thinking?" she said.

"About you."

"What about me?" she asked, almost giggling. I wanted to tell her. I wondered if I already had.

Rendering Byzantium

RENDERING BYZANTIUM

Early in March, one day into Clay Breyssee's first cycle on his new job, he awoke with a start to see his mother standing over him, holding a cup of coffee and waving the steam with dreamlike motions in his face. The shades were drawn. Clay thought, Yesterday, was it? No, today I got off and today I will be back on. Mrs. Breyssee had turned on the lamp, and she was speaking. "What?" said Clay. His ears were still ringing from the last shift. It was two o'clock, his watch on the bedside stand said: he had slept only five hours, fitfully, with an old necktie banded around his eyes and knotted in back, but it had slipped down around his throat. "Sarah's coming home," Mrs. Breyssee said, and she gave him the cup, balancing it on his chest so that he dare not doze off again lest he spill scalding coffee on his bare skin. Mrs. Breyssee left the room. Sarah Rausch, Clay's sister, was leaving her husband and returning to her mother's home. By the time she came roaring up in her car it was two-thirty, though she had promised she would be there in ten or fifteen minutes; the afternoon was overcast and dull, and Clay had trouble staying awake.

Mrs. Breyssee tried to joke, "You've all come home to roost"; and Sarah at least smiled, though Clay pretended not to hear. He had lived with his mother for the five months he was unemployed, and now that he was able to work again he was restless to move into a place of his own. Sarah arrived in her new Toyota, and as Clay trotted out to help her carry in the one suitcase she brought with her, he thought he detected a bruise on her lip. Inside the house in the electric light he thought it might be a smudge of ash, perhaps from cleaning out the fireplace. When he tried to touch the spot she winced.

The separation surprised no one. Sarah told her brother that Gordon was becoming impossible to live with: he was irritable and slovenly now that he had the new job out in the central mill lab; he would wake up during the day when he was on graveyard and wander around the apartment in his socks and sweat pants, drinking bourbon and water, or sit across the room from Sarah while she read a magazine, doing nothing but watching her and blowing smoke out of the side of his mouth. They were quarreling all the time now. Once in a fit of rage he threw a plaster horsehead bookend at the wall and shattered it (though he frightened himself as much as her). The rest, she said, was exaggerated. The fight the neighbor had reported to the police was only a loud argument. The cops arrived, and a thin officer with a freckled face talked to Sarah while his partner interviewed Gordon in the bedroom. The cop wanted to know if she wished to press any charges. Sarah said, "Like what? I told you he didn't do anything. We've just got nosy neighbors." The officer told her about restraining orders, and Sarah said she had no need of one. The policemen took their report, warned Gordon, and left.

Clay thought there had been more to it than that, but he would watch Sarah and see she did not have that empty look, and he knew that she was strong, with broad shoulders from butterfly swimming, and that she could handle herself. As a girl she had been a tomboy and liked to wrestle Clay, until one day (he was fifteen and she thirteen) she lost her temper and slugged him and ran off for several hours. "Gordon tried to talk me out of leaving," she said. "He kept telling me it isn't a permanent thing, working under this neurotic boss of his; and maybe they'll move him off rotating shift in a couple of months and he'll be himself again. I said, 'Right. I'm supposed to wait around here and watch you rage around the house like a madman for the next few months until you get a promotion? And then what? I can't live with this craziness.'"

Clay said, "They always do that: try to pressure you and talk you out of it."

"Who always says that?"

Clay caught himself and said nothing.

"What are you talking about?"

"Okay, let's drop it, Sarah," Mrs. Breyssee said. Sarah glowered at Clay, and he got up and carried her suitcase to the sewing room that had been her bedroom until she married two years ago, at eighteen.

At first Clay saw little of her. He was on graveyard for seven days straight, though unike Gordon he was union, a fifth hand on a paper winder. When he got off work at six-thirty in the morning he would walk quickly to his car, never falling in with the men who strolled along clanging their lunchboxes on the rails and chatting on the way out. He sped through the parking lot and tried to beat the rest of the traffic through the gate. Then he raced down the road along the log pond, which was stark and gray in the rain and filled with rafts of floating logs that sprouted brush and even small trees. The weather was cold, Clay felt exhilarated and happy, and as the heater warmed the car he grew drowsy and his muscles stiffened and began aching pleasurably. He was finished until that night. His mother and Sarah would be asleep when he got home, and the house would be empty and quiet. He spread out a week-old copy of the *Daily News* on the carpet and sat in a chair unlacing his boots, and he rubbed down the oxblood leather with mink oil and cleared the clots away from the seams with his fingernails. He always showered and went to bed within an hour, sometimes passing his mother on the stairway as she descended in her robe and said good morning. Clay would ask how Sarah was doing. Mrs. Breyssee would say she was not sure; Sarah had sat up in the living room smoking while the vent drew the fumes to the master bedroom. "I don't tell her it keeps me awake," Mrs. Breyssee said. "I figure she's got enough on her mind right now without her mother nagging her."

Clay lay in bed with his eyes burning and ran his fingertips lightly over the scar on his belly, not even registering the sensation on the fringes of his consciousness anymore; he told himself that if nothing else it was good to be happy for at least an hour each day, thinking, That much I can savor. And maybe mornings are the end of her nightmares too. Then he remembered and thought for a moment, abstractly, and his gut pained him. His finger twitched slightly as if pulling the trigger, four times, aiming right this time. He made himself stop. Then he listened for the sound of Sarah moving around in her room and the whine of the shower. When he heard this he stuck his earplugs in his ears and fell asleep.

The house was usually empty when Clay arose, and he stifled a sense of indignation. He would take a walk along the sidewalks striped with rows of moss, then return and watch "Perry Mason" on television or sit reading on the couch, trying to discipline himself not to look at the clock and see how much time remained before the beginning of graveyard; or he would go to his room and pour some gin from the bottle he kept on the top shelf of his closet—not that drinking mattered in theory in the Breyssee household, but the worry it would cause his mother was beyond what she should reasonably be expected to put up with in her own home. "Do you think you should be drinking alone?" she would ask. "It doesn't matter," Clay said, "I'm just having this one." Mrs. Breyssee said, "But you don't want to aggravate the bleeding in your stomach." She reached for the bottle at the foot of the couch and Clay shoved, almost kicked, her hand away. "The bleeding stopped months ago," Clay said, "back when I was still on the Santa Monica city payroll. And the bullet never even touched my damn stomach." Mrs. Breyssee raised her eyebrows and said, "Intestines, then."

Clay overslept and woke in a panic, his heart pounding, after dark. He came downstairs and found his mother serving dinner at the kitchen table. She had put out two table settings.

"Why didn't you wake me? Why did you let me sleep so late?"

"I was about to go rouse you for dinner. I didn't know you wanted to get up earlier."

"Look at the clock. It's nearly six. It's dark out. I slept ten hours."

"I'm sorry." Mrs. Breyssee stirred something on the stove. Clay averted his eyes and sat down at his place at the table. The windowpanes facing the side yard were steamed up and dark and lusterless.

"That's all right," he said. "It's not your fault. It just discourages me to get up and find I've missed the entire day and have only a few hours left before work."

Mrs. Breyssee set bowls of carrots and mashed potatoes and a platter of pork chops on the table. She sat down with him. "Well, you'll be off graveyard for a couple of weeks after tonight, won't you?"

"Yeah, that'll be nice." Clay heaped his plate with potatoes. "Where's Sarah this evening?"

"She went out." Mrs. Breyssee passed him the chops, but Clay set the platter down.

"With Gordon?"

"I think so."

"I wonder why she bothered to leave him in the first place." Mrs. Breyssee set down her knife and fork.

"I don't know," she said. "But I do know there's a lot you and I may not understand here. It's not your business to advise her what to do. The best thing you can do is keep quiet and let her reach her own decision."

Clay finished his meal and returned to his room. He lay on his bed and sketched his feet and legs, using a felt pen. His teachers in high school had told him he had a talent for drawing, and after he graduated, for want of anything better to do, he attended an art institute in Los Angeles. After two semesters he realized he was not good enough, and he dropped out and joined the police force. He drew sketches of criminals from their victims' descriptions, and one of his drawings, a rather crude and smeary one, was printed in the *Los Angeles Times.* Clay stopped drawing when he switched to being a beat cop; he had taken it up again only recently, during his convalescence. His legs looked distorted and frightening in his sketch, and he tossed the pad aside and began flipping through an oversize volume of Byzantine art that he had checked out of the library with the intent of improving his art education. Sometimes he made compositional drawings of the mosaics, with their strange borders and illustrations from the lives of the saints and prophets. He looked for a while at a scene from a basilica nave, of Abraham in the court of Abimelech. Then he went downstairs and watched television until it was time for him to leave.

Sarah and Gordon sat out on the deck, shivering in the evening air as they mixed drinks and slowly sipped them. The deck of their apartment overlooked a courtyard, and they sat at opposite ends of a swinging lounge chair, but after a few minutes Gordon got up to freshen their drinks, and when he returned he sat on the rail across from Sarah, looking like a dark piece of paper cut out in the shape of a man (she thought, A police shooting target) against the glow in the sky.

Gordon said, "Come on back. It's stupid for us to stay apart."

Sarah thought, Or more like an absence, the shape of a man simply cut out of the background, although she was aware that he was watching her.

Gordon said, "I miss you."

"I know."

"We should have been back together by now. If it wasn't for your brother we'd be back together. I think he's trying to influence you."

"Don't worry about that. I'll make up my own mind."

Gordon drained his drink. He went back in the house. This time he brought the bottle back with him.

At the end of the evening, as Sarah prepared to leave, Gordon grabbed her wrist. "Why don't you stay tonight?" he said.

"No."

Gordon said, "Kiss me, you beautiful creature, or I'll throw you down in the blackberry bramble," but he was slurring his words, and Sarah barely understood him. He was shoving her against the wooden rail. Sarah tried to break free, and slivers caught her blouse and prickled her skin. Gordon is not ugly, she thought, but he is dreadful now with his sweet fulsome scotch breath—and she worked against him, his knee between her legs, his face lurid in the amethystine glow of an electric insect killer that hung buzzing from an eave overhead. Gordon thought, When I keep her there so my shadow is off her face, the light renders her features Oriental: a face lit by the purple-black light bulb in the ceiling of the place outside the university town, near the base. "You soldier?" she asked in her faint lisp, and settling back I answered, "Yes. The army." Then she said, looking down on me, "Give me more money, soldier," and I said trembling, "All I've got is that twenty—" adding, "unless you take traveler's checks," afraid that some burly man with a yin-yang hanging between his pectorals would burst into the room and, as I attempted to hide, demand more. The woman considered, then asked, "American Express?"

Kiss her, he thought.

"One kiss and you're free," Gordon said, touching her cheeks with his fingertips. The bottle slipped from between his arm and his side, clunked on the deck, and fell with a whisper into the brush. He kissed her. She bit his lip. She tasted blood.

In the bag plant a woman named Trina Davies suffered a heart attack while tending her machine; she died a few hours later in the hospital. Reading the obituary in the newspaper, Sarah felt not only shocked but guilty, since after working in the plant on Trina's crew she had never called her and had let their friendship lapse (or at least their partnership—they had worked on the same machine but had never been close). After Sarah married Gordon, she lost touch with most of her friends in the bag plant. The funeral was held on Clay's first day off, after a seven-night stretch of graveyard, and Sarah asked him if he would drive her to the service, since her car would not start and Mrs. Breyssee was out. Clay had known Trina in high school, and he decided to attend the funeral.

They drove to the chapel of a neo-Gothic church alongside the lake in the center of town, and they hurried to the back door. They were late. The sky was cloudy, and the trees shivered in the wind. Sarah opened the door, and they saw a crowd of gray and balding heads, people neither of them knew. A union officer whose name Clay could not recall was reciting a psalm. Sarah whispered, "I don't want to go in there."

"Of course we're going in."

"No. Let's get out of here."

Clay gripped her elbow to usher her in through the door, but she shrugged him away. "Would you let go of me?" she said. Their voices and the draft from the door caused the people in the back pews to crane their necks and look back and glower, and they let the door slowly hiss closed. Clay followed Sarah to the car, hunching and squinting in the drizzle. He hopped over a puddle and unlocked her door.

"I can't believe you sometimes," he said. "Why did you ask me to bring you here if you don't even want to attend the damn funeral?"

When he got in the car Sarah was buckling her seat belt. "I don't know," she said. "I changed my mind. It seemed so terrible with that white casket and all those flowers."

"Do you want me to take you home?"

"I don't know."

Clay started the engine, and Sarah added, "Why don't we just drive around a bit?"

He drove toward the mills, where the sunlight suffused the plumes of steam. "Looks like it might clear up," he said, but Sarah was silent. They passed a muddy green field that looked like a football gridiron late in the season, a collection of wooden houses with moss growing in stripes along the rows of roof shingles, and several of the squarish, affectedly architectural churches that seem to sprout like mushrooms in small towns. A water tower was silhouetted against the radiant wisps of fog over the river. They turned on Industrial Way and drove along the raised road. To the left was a swampy slough, and on the right they passed warehouses and stacks of cut lumber with red ends and railroad cars abandoned on the tracks. A bulldozer crept about like a dung beetle on a massive pile of wood chips in the distance, and beyond, out on the wharf, Clay glimpsed a crane lifting containers onto a ship.

"Have you seen anything of Gordon at the mill?" Sarah said.

"If I have to leave the charts in the office I sometimes see him. Not usually, though."

"What was he doing?" she asked.

"I don't know."

Sarah rubbed her forearm on the window to clear away the condensation. She muttered, "You're both so jealous."

"What do you mean, jealous?"

She laughed.

They turned on Oregon Way and accelerated up the Lewis and Clark Bridge. Clay refrained from looking left at the Cowlitz Pulp and Paper Mill; the sight of it always made him feel constricted. On either side of the road ran a chain-link fence, out beyond the sidewalk and guardrail, perhaps to prevent suicides, but it stopped a hundred yards up the ramp, where the bridge began, as if the highway engineers did not mind someone quietly throwing himself off, as long as he landed beyond the piles of timber (sticks, really, from this height) intended for Japan. Loaders gathered bunches of the scuffed, barkless logs, then scurried around crazily like ants and placed their loads in piles on other parts of the wharf. Clay pointed out the fence to Sarah and laughed and said, "Anyway, if you really wanted to kill yourself, it would be better to jump straight into the river from the center of the bridge. Who would want to be crushed on the dock and have a bunch of Weyerhaeuser personnel running around and calling ambulances and trying to administer first aid to your corpse?"

"But what if you didn't die in the river? Maybe the bridge isn't high enough to kill you on impact."

"Of course it is. Look at all those little men on the ships down there."

"You still can't judge that. And if it isn't, you would probably drown slowly, whereas the whole point of jumping off a bridge is to kill yourself on impact."

Clay glanced at a truck in the rearview mirror and said, "Well, in any case I wouldn't want my body to wash up on the pilings of some abandoned fishing village, nibbled on by sturgeons. I'd rather shoot myself."

Sarah opened and closed the ashtray in her armrest. Clay looked at her. He tried to joke, "At least the fall would be a thrill."

"Really."

The Columbia River was deep and dark green, albeit dulled by the neutral tone that bled from the girders as they flashed past. The car came off the bridge, descending the ramp, and Clay turned on the highway and headed up the steep grade to the west, toward the ocean, sixty miles away. Sarah said, "Why don't you pull over at the viewpoint?"

The sky to the north was clearing, and beyond Longview and the forested ridges surrounding the town, they could see the snowy crater of Mount St. Helens, topped with a wisp of steam, and in the far distance the dome of Mount Rainier. Down on the river a tugboat churned upstream. From this height the Columbia was pale blue, except for a stripe along the far bank where the current of muddy gray water from the Cowlitz River faded into it. Clay looked upstream at the Cowlitz Mill, then looked away. Five seagoing ships were anchored at Weyerhaeuser's dock, bands of red and black floating high in the water.

"Gordon was there," Sarah said.

"Where?"

"At the funeral service, about halfway up on the right-hand side. He was looking right at us."

"What was he doing there? He never knew Trina."

"I guess he figured I would be there."

Clay nodded. Below them on the Oregon side of the river, cattle grazed on the lowlands, which were interlaced with canals and fences like the yellowing cracks on a china saucer that has been reglued. Shattered in a china shop where he fled. A few trailers were scattered in a copse along what had once been the riverbank and was now a sandy belt several hundred yards wide where the Army Corps of Engineers had pumped the spoils from the dredges, sediment washed down the Cowlitz River that filled the channel after the eruption of Mount St. Helens.

"Do you want to drive on?" Clay asked.

"Not yet."

Sarah rolled down her window and rested her arm on the back of the seat, drawing a deep breath, her bust rising and falling. Clay looked in the side mirror at a convoy of empty log trucks grinding up the hill. He turned off the ignition and got out.

A cloud bank again blocked the sun. Sarah climbed from the car and slammed her door. She rested her foot on a guardrail, although she was too short to do so comfortably. After a moment she stepped over the rail, sinking her spike heels into the soft gravelly dirt before she sat down unsteadily. Clay could smell the sulfur reek of the pulpmaking down at the mills, along with a faint whiff of her perfume. He sat on the hood, despite the fine layer of rain-spattered dirt that covered it. Sarah slid over and leaned back on his leg.

"Maybe we should leave," Clay said.

Sarah shrugged—a rising movement of her back muscles on his shin. "I like it here."

"It's a pretty view."

"You ought to paint it sometime—on a long, horizontal canvas."

"I haven't painted since I left school."

"You were drawing those pictures from the descriptions people gave you."

"I stopped doing that too."

Sarah leaned forward and brushed the hair from her eyes. Clay slid back on the hood, and when she leaned back his knee was between her shoulder blades. She looked at him.

"Let's go," he said.

"You act like you're afraid someone will see us."

"Oh, come on."

She twisted around and rested one hand on the bumper. "Why don't you like it here?"

"I hate sitting around staring at the mill on my day off. It's bad enough working there."

Sarah laughed. "All right. Since you put it that way."

She climbed over the rail and got back in the car. After a moment Clay slid from the hood and brushed off the seat of his slacks. Sarah had rolled up her window, and the air inside smelled faintly of old upholstery and antifreeze, which had leaked through the floorboard, soaking the carpet on Clay's side, but they continued to sit and stare into the distance.

Sarah said, "I came here with Gordon once."

Clay dug in his pocket for his keys. His sister was looking upstream, toward the Cowlitz River, where a long sandbar stuck into the Columbia.

"Mom said you had dinner with him the other day."

"Yep. If he wouldn't drink it wouldn't be so bad."

"It's always that way."

"You're the expert. We had a couple of cops come and talk to us once; I think I told you about that. I tried to imagine you doing that, but I couldn't."

Clay smiled. "I found those situations odd, myself. You always think of yourself as a nice guy with a mom and a sister and a few friends, and then you find someone waving a hunting knife at you and threatening to kill you. I never could understand it."

"That's not how it was with us when the cops came."

Sarah picked up her purse and absently rummaged through it. "This isn't the first time I've left him," she said. "We separated just before you got shot, but we didn't tell you about it because you were in the hospital and Mom said it would tear you apart inside while you were supposed to be recuperating. Actually, I thought it would cheer you up. But by the time you were out we were back together, and there was no need to say anything about it."

"Don't be stupid. You know that wouldn't cheer me up. I just don't want him to do something to you."

"I can take care of myself. If I leave him for good it's just because we don't have any feeling for each other anymore. Sometimes I think the police colored your view of every relationship around you. Not every couple that argues ends up shooting each other."

Clay glowered darkly, and Sarah said, "Okay?" and touched his arm. He said nothing, and she opened the glove compartment and flipped it closed.

Clay looked at her, but she ignored him.

"Why don't we keep driving toward the beach?" she suggested.

Clay started the car, backed around, and drove across the gravel roadside onto the highway back to Longview.

As they came in the door, Mrs. Breyssee met them in the kitchen and said Gordon had called. Sarah shoved past her and walked back to her room. "Sarah, what's wrong?" her mother said. Her door slammed.

Just after ten o'clock, as Clay dressed for work and stuck his paper knife in its leather sheath in his hip pocket, he heard a crash in the room where Sarah was staying. He knocked on the door. "Are you all right?" he asked. Sarah said, "Yes, I'm fine. A lamp just fell over." Clay heard shuffling and something clinking in the room. He asked, "Can I help you? Did it break?" Sarah said, "Just bring me a dustpan and leave it by the door, please." He brought a dustpan and broom and leaned them against the wall, adjusted their angle, and listened for a moment. All was silent. Perhaps she was listening too. He trod back down the warped wooden floor to the kitchen, where he put on his work boots. Walking out on the back porch, he saw that the light in her room was out, and one shade was bunched around the edge, as though someone was peeking around it. The light came on in the kitchen, and through the filmy curtain he saw Sarah moving about, fetching herself a glass of water.

Fourteen days after Clay started at Cowlitz, a letter arrived in the mail threatening him with dismissal if he failed to get a checkup with the company doctor. "Its' [*sic*] only because of an oversight that you were allowed to work this long without a checkup and/or attending jitney drivers school (circle one)," the form letter explained. Clay went to see the doctor, whose office was painted the same dull green as everything else at the mill. A nurse with faint mustaches on either side of her mouth handed him a form to fill out, and he sat down across from the other two people in the waiting room, a young man with a thin beard over his pock-scarred face and a woman who covered her upper lip with her tongue as she scribbled a comment beside one of the questions on her form.

The questionnaire requested information on the employee's family history of illness (syphilis? neuromuscular disorders? scrofula?); Clay checked epilepsy (his father) and allergies (Uncle Phil, pistachio nuts). Another question requested information about the employee's own "diseases, illnesses, injuries, or conditions: check the ones that apply." Clay left them all blank, including the one about suicidal tendencies or wishes, thinking, None of your damn business, and if I sometimes consider how it would have been had he aimed a little higher and (from his perspective) to the right—if I imagine the second shot missing my heart, unreasonably, at a distance of ten feet, and almost wish it had been fired a few degrees higher—it's nothing they need to know to evaluate whether I'm strong enough to be a fifth hand in a mill.

A nurse called, "Clay, you're next."

She directed him through a door, and he headed down the hall, stepping aside to let a fat man with a grizzled beard pass. A white-haired doctor opened the sliding door of an examination room, and Clay entered. The doctor gestured toward a chair and removed the questionnaire from Clay's hand. "So, you're working in the central mill, huh?" he asked. Clay sat down and said, "Yes." His hands were in his lap and he saw that his fingers were smeared with blood. Blood spattered his pants legs.

He said, "It looks like I've cut my finger."

The doctor scowled at Clay's hands. "You'd better wash your hands in the sink there. I'll get you a Band-Aid."

"Thanks."

Clay soaped his hands with a liquid carrying a strong medicinal smell and dried them on a grainy paper towel. The doctor, an old man with a baggy, flushed face, took Clay's fingers in his pink hand and applied the Band-Aid.

"Were you picking at your fingernail out in the waiting room?"

"I guess so."

"Well, don't tear at your nails like that. It' a good way to get an infection."

"All right."

The doctor sat on a chair at the foot of an examining table covered with thin white paper.

"Where are you from, Clay? This area?"

"Yeah, originally. I've been living in LA for a couple of years, though."

"Oh, really? My wife and I own a vacation home in Redondo Beach."

"Nice area."

"So," the doctor said. "How's your health been this past year?"

"Good."

"Any injuries of any kind?"

"No."

"I notice you're on Imipramine. Are you still? Hmm." The doctor scratched his eyebrow with a pen. "What is Imipramine? I don't quite recall."

"It's an antidepressant."

"Really? Yes, of course. Why did you let yourself get so down in the mouth that you needed medication?"

Clay looked at the old man in surprise.

"I was a police officer, and I was involved in some shootings, and it got me down," thinking, It would only confuse you to explain: the woman leaving her house and running into her former husband, who waited in her carport with a box of candy, shoving it at her, losing his temper, and slapping her when she refused to take it, before I heard the call on the radio and responded and pulled up and he became frightened and shot her once through the head with a .357 Magnum and then shot me in the gut, knocking me back into the patrol car, and he ran and hid in a china shop while the medics cut away my shirt and pricked me in their haste. How that might render a man unable to work for five months after a doctor pronounced him healed. How he might spend every day pondering (though with diminishing intensity) the angles of trajectory and the speed with which he had squeezed off the bullets, none of which, not a single one, had found home, struck flesh, avenged.

The doctor laughed once and his pupils dilated. "How hard did you look for another job? Of course you're going to see shootings and such as a law officer. If I prescribed antidepressants for every medic who's seen an industrial accident, why we'd have a bunch of drug fiends running around here."

Clay stared at him.

The doctor said, "Well." He coughed and shuffled Clay's papers. "Are you still taking this medication?"

"Yes."

The old man dropped his gaze to the papers and said, "Hmm," scribbled a note and again said, "Hmm." He looked up and smiled, flashing his false teeth, and said, "Okay. That'll be about it."

He handed Clay the papers, and as Clay left the room, the doctor called, "You'd better watch it about that cut, getting blood all over yourself like that; we may have to list you as an accident risk."

Clay was walking toward the door and did not look back. He glanced at what was written on his record before returning the papers to the nurse. Scrawled at the bottom of one page in felt pen was "health good," underlined twice.

Clay worked for the first few weeks on machines Six or Nine. The machines, three stories high and nearly three hundred feet long, were in an enormous, low-ceilinged hall with cinderblock walls and bricked-up windows—except for a few glass tiles in the wall above one end of Six, which were so thickly coated with dust that they were invisible at night and only gave off a dim blue glow during the day. Number Seven was in a different room, and Clay could see part of the machine through a huge doorway, the corrugated steel panels of its sides bathed, at unpredictable times, in an unearthly emerald light. One swing shift he was assigned to Seven. To his surprise the room was huge and expansive, with a high ceiling like a cathedral nave. The room was bright, and daylight filtered through its green fiberglass walls, which were supported by square columns. When the sun set the walls were ablaze with light. Steam rose like incense from the wet end of the machine, where the liquid pulp was sprayed on a broad belt before the sheet ran the length of the dryer. Once Clay saw a dove soaring high in the din from the machine, suffused with light, gliding in the steam.

On the rare sunny afternoons, Clay would climb the stairway to the roof and sit out under the bright hazy sky and look at the river, the port, the trains crashing and locking together on the tracks leading to the mill docks below. Usually, however, it was rainy and bleak and cold this time of year. Machine Seven ran slower than the other two in the central mill, and the workers had fifteen minutes' break for every forty-five they worked, while they waited for the machine to catch up with them. One day Gordon wandered through the room, while the men sat around the third hand's glassed-in booth, and waved at Clay. "Who the fuck's that?" asked Bruce, an enormously overweight fourth hand with a long ponytail and a shaggy mustache and a gut that hung over his belt. Clay said, "My brother-in-law." He went outside to talk to Gordon. Gordon was wearing a shirt and tie and slacks, and he looked out of place among the men in their glue-stiffened jeans and holey baseball shirts. He said, "Can I talk to you in the crew room for a second?"

Clay followed him to the crew room, which was located right off the Number Seven work area. He pulled a handkerchief from his pocket and wiped the grimy sweat from his face. Four flat, long tables were shoved together in the center of the room, surrounded by folding chairs. Gordon sat on a table, and Clay sat in a chair and removed his earplugs.

"How's it going?" said Gordon.

"Not bad. It's a pretty slow day. What are you up to these days?"

"Not a whole lot. Just working and hanging around the apartment." Gordon pulled over a chair and rested his feet on it. "I was wondering if you'd like to grab a beer after work today."

Clay glanced at the chalkboard, where someone had written, "Injury free days: 3," and said, "Thanks, but I'd rather not on swing shift. I'm always so tired when I get off, and I'd just as soon go to bed."

Gordon shrugged. "Sure, I understand. It's just that I sometimes have trouble sleeping right after work, and it's kind of nice to unwind a bit."

Clay nodded, and Gordon looked away. He gripped the table with both hands. "How come you two ran out when you saw me in church the other day?"

Clay flushed. "She didn't want to see you."

"Figures."

"Why were you there?"

"I used to work with Trina's father. He was a pretty good friend for a while. Sarah probably told you I didn't even know her."

"No, she didn't."

Gordon crossed his arms. "How is she doing?"

"Fine, I guess. I don't see that much of her."

"Is she still having trouble sleeping?"

"I don't know."

"She told me she's not sleeping well. It's the same thing with me. I woke up the other night, and I sat in the living room shivering but too lazy to turn up the heater. I read for a couple of hours. By the time I went to bed it was four o'clock, and I still lay in bed thinking for a half hour or so."

"That's too bad."

"Has she said anything about me?"

"No."

"She told me you were acting like a detective, checking out her face and telling her how I was sounding like a typical criminal or something. I might not have gotten your words exactly right, but you know what I'm talking about. Don't talk to her like that. Let her make up her own mind."

"Have you ever hit her?"

Gordon blinked. "Don't be stupid. Of course not."

The buzzer sounded; the reel of paper turned over, and it was time for Clay to return to work.

Gordon hopped off the table and opened the door for Clay, and a blast of hot air met them. He said, "Would you mind not telling her I talked to you?"

"Why?"

"Oh, come on. I know you don't like me, but you can do that much. Aw, go ahead. I don't care."

Clay shrugged. "All right." He rolled his earplugs and stuffed them back in his ears, and he could not hear what Gordon said as they walked off.

After Clay got off work he parked for a few minutes by the millpond. He stared down the road at a group of abandoned mills, which resembled an armada of men-of-war wrecked on the shore and left to rot. The rearview mirror reflected the sky over the mill, the dull orange steam suffused with the lights of the buildings. An enormous pile of wood chips, held back with a forty-foot-high retaining wall braced with timbers, blocked his view of most of the buildings. A string of headlights approached from the direction of the mill and passed with dull howling noises. Clay was wide awake, and he decided to go for a drink on his own.

The bar was crowded, and Clay stayed for several hours. One of the waitresses, Sandy, kept watching him, and he smiled at her. She waved. When she got a break she came over to his table and sat down opposite him. Sandy was young and pretty, and she had a brother who she said was a cop in Kelso. She had only been working here a few months.

"Where have you been, Clay? I haven't seen you for a while."

"I've been working."

"No kidding? You got a job? That's great. Where?"

"Cowlitz."

"That's wonderful. How long have you been there?"

"A few weeks."

"Don't become a stranger, though. We miss you around here."

A logger at a nearby table was looking at them. He wore red suspenders, and his jeans had been snipped off above the ankles. He hollered, "Hey, girl, are you a waitress? I need another pitcher."

Sandy said, "Hang on a second." Then she told Clay, "I've got to get back to work. Give me a call sometime."

"Sure."

She wiped down his table with a wet rag and left.

When Clay came home he found Sarah in the living room, leafing through his sketchpad.

"Don't look at those drawings," he said.

Sarah slid the sketchpad across the floor in his direction, and it went under the couch. "You're late," she said.

Clay pulled his shoes off and ignored her.

She persisted, "You smell like beer."

"I'm not your husband. You don't have to nag me."

"I'm not nagging. I was just commenting."

"Right." Clay yawned. "I stopped at a tavern after work and had a few drinks. Somebody spilled a pitcher on me." He sat on the floor in front of the couch. "What are you doing up?"

"Oh, I woke up about midnight and couldn't get back to sleep." Sarah combed her fingers through her hair.

"Mind if I play a record?"

"No, that's fine. Just don't wake Mom."

Clay selected a record of Bach's harpsichord music from his mother's collection. Sarah said, "Oh, don't play that. Play blues or something."

He pulled the lever to start the record. "I've been listening to the jukebox all night in the bar, and I feel like something different. Oh, I was going to tell you: I heard this incredible story from an old man in the bar. You interested? The guy who told it is named Carson; he's this bearded fat man in a polyester suit who sat chugging pitchers as fast as people would buy them for him. When he took off his jacket, his arms were tattooed with swastikas and dragons and naked women. It was the oddest thing. I overheard him at a table near mine, talking to a group that included a Rastafarian in dreadlocks. I slid my chair closer. Other people in the bar eventually stopped talking, and pretty soon quite a few stragglers were listening. At first I thought the people at his table were just laughing at him, but I began to realize they were maybe a little afraid of him."

"Okay, go on," said Sarah. She hugged her knees and tucked her nightgown around her feet.

"Am I boring you?" Clay asked.

"No. Go ahead."

"The story he told is about a man Carson met maybe ten years ago, in a jail in West Palm Beach in Florida. Carson was almost proud of having been in jail; he said, 'I ain't lying. I robbed a liquor store with a sawed-off shotgun.' Someone at the bar laughed and said, 'You'd better watch out what you're saying, old man. Breyssee here is an excop.' So Carson turned and looked back at me and said, 'I won't give nobody—cop or no cop—any apology for the poverty and anguish and fear that drives a man to stick the barrel of a gun in somebody's belly and threaten to kill him in exchange for a drawerful of small bills. Or to stick a gun in his own mouth.' I smiled and said nothing but thought, I wish I had been the cop to bust up that robbery.

"Carson's friend was named Masterson. They shared a jail cell with about forty other men. Masterson would read a lot and sit on his bunk, ignoring the poker games and fights and yelling, but Carson got to know him, and Masterson eventually began telling about this tropical island he had lived on for about five years. He had embezzled some money from the firm where he worked, and he went to this island where his old college roommate was a missionary, because the place seemed far enough away to be safe, and the missionary friend was always writing about how wonderful the climate was and how cheaply you could live there: you could eat fresh mangoes and papayas and coconuts every day and live in a decent house with a couple of servants to cook and do laundry for you for practically nothing. Masterson was especially impressed with a cheap local rum called Little Cock in the native tongue. Yeah, I see you smiling—that's what we were thinking; everyone in the bar was laughing. But he said the rum was named for fighting cocks.

"Cockfighting is the national sport of this island. The men bring their roosters to a ring set up on the outskirts of a village, and they drink rum and size up their birds, letting them fly at each other and pulling them back by a string that they attach to the bird's ankle. One little old blind woman sells shots of rum to the men, and they sit around gambling and playing board games if they don't have fighting cocks."

"They wouldn't keep me away, if I was there."

"What?"

"They'd have to put up with a woman, because I'd be curious."

"Yeah, and you'd be conspicuous too. This Masterson told Carson he stood out like a sore thumb, the only white man there. I can imagine what it would be like to be a white woman. Anyway, Carson said they strip the feathers at the ends of the cocks' wings, leaving only the quills. They sharpen the quills with penknives and then tuck the roosters under their arms and whittle the birds' spurs razor-sharp. Just before the fight, the owners take a mouthful of rum and cloves and spit all over the cocks, in their faces, under their wings, on their bodies, and the birds are infuriated—they flap their wings and shriek. When the owners release the cocks, they attack each other while the men bet and hand money back and forth. Masterson said before long he had a cock brought to him from Georgia that could beat anybody's, tear the poor birds to shreds and leave them limp and bloody and gasping in the center of the ring.

"Masterson's missionary friends—they were named something like Smith or Jones. Smith, I guess. The Smiths lived in the capital city. They were under the impression that Masterson had made a killing on the stock market, but they didn't ask many questions. Masterson's buddy Carl Smith drank a lot, to the point that the other missionaries were beginning to talk. Their neighbors sometimes heard shouts and crashing around at night."

Sarah scraped the side of her foot on the carpet.

Clay said, "I don't know. That's what Carson said. When Masterson was in town, he used to drop in on them, take a dip in the pool, and spend the afternoon talking with Smith's wife. She would pad around the pool barefoot in her bathing suit, dipping eucalyptus leaves out of the water with a net. Masterson would watch her and think that despite the stretch marks on her belly she was very lovely, and if she glanced at him he would keep looking at her and she would turn away. When Smith came home they would all sit up on the terraced rooftop, under a canopy of wisteria that grew over a trellis. They drank rum liqueurs while the sun set over the bay and the roofs of the slums down on the lowlands by the wharf grew rosy and the shadows deepened between the shanties. Maybe Smith would say, 'It must be nice to have the money to retire at your age.'

"And Masterson would say, 'I can't complain. I don't lack much,' glancing at Mrs. Smith.

"Smith said, 'A lot of poor people you see (that woman living in the shack built against the wall of the alley, for example) would love to have even a tenth of your money or mine to throw around. No, not to throw around—to buy rice and beans for her children and a small home and a dress that's not ripping open at the seams.'

"'I know,' Masterson said. 'I talk to them every day. They beg me for money every time I step out my front door. Sometimes they get impatient when I am away, and they try to borrow from my abundance.'

"'They're desperate. They're starving.'

"Masterson grimaced and flicked his cigarette butt at a green lizard sunning on the ledge of the building. He hated this kind of talk.

"One day Masterson dropped in on his friends, and Mrs. Smith insisted he stay for dinner. She was busy rearranging the furniture with one of the servants because they were having a party that night, so she said, 'You're practically family, Robert. You won't be offended if I ask you to head on in to the kitchen and fix yourself a drink?'

"He went back to the kitchen, a long, narrow, hot room at the back of the house. The cook, a fat woman in a headscarf, was getting a stained package of meat out of the refrigerator, and Masterson reached past her and helped himself to a pitcher of punch. Then the cook stepped aside, cradling the meat like a baby. She grinned, gap-toothed, at Masterson and greeted him in the native tongue. Masterson smiled and asked what was for dinner. The cook unwrapped a beautiful bloody tenderloin. She set it on the chopping block and began to carve it for chateaubriand, in thin slices lightly marbled with fat.

"'What do you call that?' Masterson asked.

"The cook looked puzzled. 'Beef,' she said.

"Masterson said, 'Well, where does that cut come from?' The cook smiled and made a carving motion with her knife along her side. Carson demonstrated the gesture this evening like this: slicing away at his pudgy side. Everyone around the table was quiet, and he glowered, waiting for someone to contradict him. Then he said, 'The cook told him it is very fine meat,' and he sipped his beer and looked up at the clock hanging over the bar. No one spoke. Carson kept on talking.

"Dinner that night was fine, but Masterson said the meat

was a little off. So was all the meat they ate there, of course; but it reminded Masterson of moose, which he had eaten when he worked in British Columbia. He thought nothing of it, since you always saw slabs of ribs hanging in the marketplace, covered with flies in the hundred-degree weather. This wasn't where the foreigners and well-off locals bought their meat, but you learned not to ask questions about the source of your food."

"Okay," said Sarah.

"No, this is funny," Clay said. "Masterson even tried to take photos once of a butcher in an open-air market, hacking away at a carcass with a cleaver. But when the butcher noticed the white man with the camera, he shook his cleaver at Masterson. I guess he didn't mind you eating the stuff; he just preferred you didn't say where you got it.

"The dinner was pleasant. Smith was sober, their kid behaved well, and their guests, who were building a dam for a village up in the mountains, turned out to be interesting people.

"The next day Masterson drove his Jeep back to the country, where he told Carson you lived even more cheaply than in the capital. He didn't hear from the Smiths for more than a month. One day he strolled down to the dusty village near his house to pick up his mail from a Methodist minister who ran a mission there and who had just returned from the capital. There was a letter from Mrs. Smith. He read it walking home, squinting at the bright paper in the sun and sometimes stumbling over the ruts. She said they were returning to the States because Smith's health problems made it impossible for them to continue their work there. She referred to a visit by the local gendarmes, perhaps (the letter was unclear at this point) called in by the Smiths' neighbors. Mrs. Smith concluded that they might be able to find some help for Smith in the United States.

"The next morning Masterson made the eight-hour trip

along the dirt roads back to the capital. When he arrived, early in the afternoon, the only people at home were the cook and the Smiths' boy. The cook said Mrs. Smith would be back in half an hour, and would he like to wait? She brought Masterson a Rob Roy, and he sat in a wicker chair and savored the breeze coming through the iron-barred windows of a room on the ground floor at the front of the house.

"The boy came barreling into the room in his school uniform. He stopped dead, holding a plastic bag filled with grass clippings.

" 'Hi, Mr. Masterson,' he said.

"And Masterson says, 'Hey, kid. How's it going?'

" 'We're leaving for America next week.'

" 'I know, that's why I came to visit. Are you sorry to be going?'

"The boy shrugged. Then he said. 'Want to see my snake?' He smiled shyly and twisted the top of his plastic bag. Masterson said, 'Sure,' so the boy brought the bag over. The strange thing was, Carson told us, leaning on his elbows and almost hissing his words, the snake seemed to be biting its own tail, devouring itself.

" 'When are you and your folks heading out?' Masterson asked, but the boy said nothing; he was preoccupied, dancing the snake around on the furniture. Then the boy said, 'We ate people before.'

"Masterson figured the boy was pulling his leg, so he just said, 'What do you know!'

"The boy went on, 'The meat we ate last time you were here was people. Daddy cried when he found out.'

"Masterson said, 'Heck, that's just my luck. That makes it the second time this month somebody's served me people without telling me,' thinking, The kid might be joking, but it's obvious that Smith ain't the only one in this household with problems.

"But Masterson said the boy seemed to believe him. The

kid said, 'We served it to all the guests that night. And Mommy made the leftovers into sandwiches and a casserole.'

"Masterson said, 'Was it a good casserole?'

"'It was okay. It had broccoli in it.'

"'Where did your mom get the people?'

"'Mom didn't buy it. Celeste the cook did, from a butcher shop. There was this crazy man who would invite people to parties—poor people, so no one would notice they were missing. And when he had picked out the fattest people in the crowd he invited them to a room where he had a secret trap-door, and when no one was looking he would pull a lever, and the guests would fall through the floor. And the man would kill them and sell the meat to a butcher up on the hill in the nice part of town. That's where Celeste bought our meat. The police arrested the man and closed the shop when they found out.'

"Masterson said, 'Why did he do that?'

"The boy said, 'I already told you he was crazy.'"

Sarah said, "That's disgusting."

"No kidding. Carson said Masterson felt nauseated, even though he still didn't believe the boy. He said, 'How did they catch the murderer?'

"The boy said, 'He tried to jump a plainclothes cop. The cop almost threw him down the hole before the man gave up. It turned out the man's cellar had sixty skeletons in it, and they brought some policemen over from the States to help identify them. Everyone said the man had powerful magic to enchant people, but our cook says his magic wasn't very strong or he would have turned them into animals first. She said that's what happened at this sacred waterfall out in the country. A farmer was missing for a week, and then a witch doctor showed up for a feast with a bull he was going to slaughter. But when he led the bull into the waterfall and hacked its head off, it screamed out in a man's voice. Every-one knew it was the guy, but they couldn't do anything because the witch doctor's magic was so strong. I don't know if they ate him, though.'"

Sarah said, "I don't believe that."

"Of course not," said Clay. "No, I mean I don't think the boy said that—if there even was a boy. I think Masterson made it up."

"I don't know," Clay said. "But Carson said he made the same objection in jail, and Robert Masterson just sat there on the edge of a sink, staring at the black spots on the floor where the carpet had been glued until an inmate managed to unravel a strip and hang himself. Someone in the bar—this potbellied man with a mustache—started saying, 'If this Masterson was so rich and had it so good in the Philippines or wherever, how come he returned to America and got himself thrown in jail?'

"Carson told him, 'I never said nothing about his being rich. I said he was living there because the living was cheap. And he came back after Carl tried to drown his wife. Masterson was in love with her. Now, maybe love isn't something someone as ugly as yourself understands—'

"Everyone laughed, and the guy shut up. But Masterson, on his island, heard Smith's voice booming out from the other room. The boy jumped up. Smith said, 'You come in here this instant.' The boy ran to his father. Masterson heard Smith say in a low voice, 'Why did you tell him that fool tale?' There was a pause, maybe while the kid made excuses, and Masterson swirled the ice in his glass to remind Smith he was there and overhearing everything. Smith said, 'I thought I told you that story was a lie. Didn't I? Answer me! Well, I guess we know what that makes you, hmm? Speak up! A liar, that's right.' As Smith kept yelling, Masterson got the feeling that the man had listened from the hall the entire time, waiting for his boy to finish the story.

"Then Mrs. Smith burst in the door. She rushed through the den where Masterson was waiting, and she ran down the hall and spoke soothingly to her husband in the other room. Smith said, almost pleading, 'But he told the whole story about the meat.'

"Mrs. Smith said, 'You, get on out of here,' and then, 'Who did he tell? For heaven's sake, how did he learn about that?' "Smith said, 'I don't know how he found out. Maybe from the cook. But he just told your boyfriend, Robert Masterson.' His wife said, 'Don't talk like that. How could he tell him anyway?' "Smith said, 'Masterson's here. Didn't you see him as you came in?' Then Mrs. Smith lowered her voice, and after a few minutes she returned to the room where Masterson was waiting. She was trembling, and she told Masterson that her husband had been under tremendous pressure for some time, and he was rather short-tempered these days; she said not to believe the kid: the meat was fine, and the boy was having these horrible vivid fantasies and getting ideas from the cook. She started to cry. Masterson held her, and she wept on his shoulder. This was the only time he ever held her, he told Carson. He felt her rib cage expanding and contracting against his chest and her mouth gasping on his neck, until finally she settled down and stepped back and dabbed at her eyes with a tissue she fished from her pocket.

"'I'm sorry,' she said. 'This isn't a very good time for us.'

"'Of course,' said Masterson. 'I'll leave now.'

"Mrs. Smith touched his arm and said, 'I know you don't believe in this, but please pray for us.'

"'I will,' said Masterson, and he walked out the door and up the broken concrete driveway to the front gate. It was locked. The boy ran up with the key and let him out.

"Masterson said he told the story to some of his friends from that country, and they said it was true: someone had been selling human flesh as meat, although they hastened to add that such a thing was as unheard of in their country as in Canada, where they supposed Masterson was from.

"When Carson finished his story, the whole bar was quiet, and he sat there patiently until somebody realized he wanted a beer, and in the commotion as they passed it to his table somebody dumped half of it on me. So I came home. They were about to close anyway."

For several minutes they were silent. Sarah picked at a thread where a button was missing on the armrest of her chair. Clay lay on his back on the floor and surveyed the strange architecture of the ceiling, like the foundations of a great city, razed and viewed from the air.

Sarah slid from her chair and sat on the floor and said, "That's as bad as some of your police stories."

Clay smiled. You filled your mug from the coffeepot boiled brackish at the end of the shift and told stories, perhaps remarked on each other's cases as you had heard them over the radio. There was Edel, who had dyslexia but who knew how to fill out a police report because he could recognize the words in context; he told about the man beating his common-law wife and setting her atop the stove, the burner coil glowing; how her robe caught fire and she tore it from her body and fled naked from the house, which, Edel told them and even repeated later in court, didn't burn down only by a miracle, in that her husband knocked a pan of boiling string beans from the stove, dousing her burning robe, as he pursued her. Stumbling, drunk ("highly intoxicated," Edel would write), the man chased her until she hid in a tree laden with ripe avocados in a neighbor's yard, and her husband fell asleep in a sandbox. The others laughed when Edel told his story—not that they were callous, but you could keep your job and prevent such things from happening only by assuming a sort of distant irony.

Clay rubbed his eyes with his palms so hard that swarms of nervelike specks whirled in his field of vision, and he thought of the poetry his father had loved to recite, of Yeats' wishful lie, "Words alone are certain good."

"What?" said Sarah.

"Nothing." Clay continued to explore the planes and inverted arch of the ceiling and doorway.

Sarah lay on her stomach on the floor across from him, propped up on her elbows. She rested her chin on her hands. "You're hard to read," she said.

Clay shrugged, agitated.

He was slowly overwhelmed with horror, and a series of images clicked past cyclically, each chamber empty: the crushed Styrofoam hamburger box on the floor of the car, the suds on the pavement—washed down by the time the television crew arrived—the sight of Sykora's goddamn shiny shaven head as he nonchalantly fled. Clay seemed (in the living room, now) to be viewing the two of them from above, his own face staring back at him, fully aware. He fancied the image doubled infinitely, as in two mirrors facing each other, and dread filled his soul. Surrender to the soldiers who have brought down our city. Confess to this heresy. Then the illusion passed, and he felt weak.

"What's the matter?" Sarah said.

"Nothing."

"You look sick."

"I had this strange feeling come over me, but I'm okay."

"You aren't thinking about that police stuff, are you?" she asked. "Didn't your doctor say not to keep replaying those things in your mind?"

"I'm not."

The record was playing again, and Clay rolled over and lifted the needle and turned it off. Sarah sat up.

"Did Gordon beat you?" he asked.

"No." She looked away and rubbed her left eye.

"Why did you have that bruise on your face when you moved back here?"

"I don't know. I bumped myself somehow."

"Clumsy you."

Sarah stared at him, her eyes glistening. "All right," she said. "He slugged me a couple of times. He never did anything like that before—not when I left him the first time. It's just when he's on this shift and he starts drinking—"

A tear trickled down her cheek, and Clay offered his handkerchief.

"Did you fight back?"

"Don't be stupid."

"You used to fight me."

"That was different and you know it. Besides, it all happened so quick and then it was over, and we were standing there panting and glaring at each other."

"Why didn't you tell the cops? Or call me? I would have beaten the hell out of him."

"I know, that's what scares me. You'd kill him. Besides, it only lasted a few minutes. All of a sudden he was apologizing and crying, and by the time the cops got to our place it was more embarrassing than anything else."

"So of course you forgave him."

Sarah wiped her eyes and said, "I left, didn't I?"

"Then you're through with him?"

"I don't know. I still keep hoping."

"For what?"

"I don't know. Maybe when he gets off rotating shift he'll be himself again."

"Sarah."

"It's not hopeless."

Sarah was often out now, and she made a point of being away when Clay was home. She saw more of Gordon, took walks with him, went to Portland with him and watched a karate movie. They ate at a motel restaurant on the Columbia before the show; she ordered wine, but Gordon did not drink. She asked, "Don't you want a glass of wine with your steak?"

"Don't tempt me."

"What do you mean?"

The waitress was tapping her pen on her notebook, and Gordon said, "Thanks, that'll be all." She left. He said, "I'm not drinking anymore. I know how it bothers you when I—well, I don't think I really get plastered that often, if ever. I'm a big guy, and at my weight you can handle your drinks pretty well. But I don't want to do something that worries you."

"Maybe I shouldn't drink. We can still catch the waitress."

"Oh, no. I don't care at all. Really. The thing is, I want you back." Gordon leaned forward and rested his chin on his fist, his elbow in the goose liver pâté.

Sarah laughed. "You're such a romantic."

He smiled and reddened and brushed the pâté from his elbow. "I'm such a klutz," he said. "I feel like I'm courting you all over again."

She sighed. "Gordon, Gordon."

"I can control my temper. It won't be the same." Gordon picked a piece of pâté from his elbow and popped it in his mouth, grinning. He had such a disarming smile.

"Nothing's the same," Sarah said. "Nothing."

"What are you going to do—stay with your mom forever?"

"I don't know. I don't want to talk about it."

"We have to talk about it sometime."

"Not now. Let's just enjoy the evening. Pretend we were never married."

"Then I can try for you again."

Sarah looked out the window at the lights on the river and said nothing.

The crew shut down Six to repair the wet end, and the foreman told Clay to remove some panels on the back side of the machine. Clay climbed along a slippery edge covered with wet pulp, yanking loose the panels. It was a three-story drop to the concrete floor where jitneys were scuttling about. The foreman came up a ladder and said, "Hey, not those. Get back from there. You'll kill yourself." As Clay moved away his foreman said, "You got more guts than me." Half an hour later Superintendent Kent called Clay into his office. He gestured toward a swivel chair, sat down himself, and smiled painfully. "You know, Clay, the men you work with have been saying they're concerned about you. I've watched you myself and I know what they mean. You don't seem comfortable around machines. Most people adjust after a few months, but you haven't done so. You keep getting yourself in dangerous situations. You seem preoccupied. And it's not just that incident this afternoon. I hear you walked under a twenty-ton crane lifting a reel of paper without batting an eye. Unless you're a born-again Christian and you're all prayed up, I wouldn't recommend that." Clay smiled. Kent lifted his hands and dropped them to his knees. "I don't know what to say, because I've never had a man before who didn't have a sense of danger. Your application says you used to be a cop. You must know what I'm talking about. Anyway, if you keep looking like an accident risk, we're going to have to let you go."

After work, Clay drove to a dirt lot behind a car wash at the corner of Oregon Way and Industrial Way, at the foot of the bridge. The intersection was busy all night as log trucks ground past, and the air was filled with the din of the loaders in the Weyerhaeuser yard. Clay stood at the corner as a lone railroad engine rumbled through the intersection and sounded its horn, halting traffic; the trembling pavement tickled the soles of his feet. The train passed through the intersection, which was littered with wood chips, and headed into the darkness in the direction of the Cowlitz Pulp and Paper Mill. The engine became a blinking constellation drawing closer and closer together. Then it rounded a bend in Industrial Way and the lights vanished. The stoplight turned green, and Clay crossed the street.

He headed up the ramp to the bridge, passing a sign that read, "Danger: Sidewalk Closed Ahead." The fence beyond the guardrail was topped with barbed wire, and as Clay continued up the incline he saw that the fence followed the ramp at the edge of the road, then dropped away as the bridge left the earth, and even entered the water beside the wharf and encircled a small floating dock. His perspective on the Weyerhaeuser plant grew: acres of logs on the dock, loaders darting about, mills dotted with yellow lights. A Japanese freighter with a red-and-green hulk and a white superstructure was moored to the dock and a cluster of pilings leaning inward like tepee poles.

The road narrowed as Clay ascended the bridge. He passed another sign: "Sidewalk Closed, Unsafe, Extreme Hazard." The newspaper had said that a pedestrian crossing the bridge had discovered the danger when his leg broke through a hole in the sidewalk, and he found himself with a skinned shin and a pounding heart, watching pebbles of concrete tumble slowly hundreds of feet into the water. Clay walked in the gutter. A truck roared past and blasted its horn, and the bridge shook and trembled. A swirl of grit and dust stung his eyes.

Clay continued walking, wondering how far it was to the top. It looked like it was about to level off. A pickup truck roared past, and a man in the passenger seat wearing a cowboy hat yelled, "Get off the road, idiot!" and threw a bottle. Clay ducked. The bottle sailed over the rail and vanished. A low mist blanketed the Columbia. The Longview side was brightly lit (the white superstructure of the ship, the timberyard, the light-flecked darkness of the city itself), but ahead, toward the Oregon bank, the hills were dark save for the headlights and taillights of cars ascending and descending the grade past the Rainier vista point. The bridge began leveling out. He came to the midpoint and halted.

Clay stepped onto the sidewalk and leaned on the rail, locking his fingers together, measuring the level of the river against the markings on the freighter's hull: maybe two meters deep. The empty ship floated high in the water. Pilings dotted with flashing red lights protected the bulwarks of either foot of the bridge. You would only need to lunge forward. Finish off Sykora's job seven months later. And he will be out in a few years. Kent would not be surprised: "Did you read the *Daily News* about Breyssee? Thank God he didn't throw himself in the hydropulper." If you had seen the gun in Sykora's hand as you pulled into the driveway. If you had called "Sykora" and as he started said, "Drop it or I'll shoot." The suspect raised his weapon and prepared to shoot and I squeezed off three rounds thereby hitting him in the neck and twice in the head and causing his demise. How could you fail to see it? Of course there was the dumpster, and his back had to be turned just right so you did not notice the angle of his arm and elbow. But those .357s are so damn big. Green used to keep one at home wrapped in newspaper, and the day we drank all those beers he said, "Would you like to see it?" and you said, "I don't like playing with guns when I'm drunk." Green laughed and insisted, "We're not playing. Damn it, we're cops." He got it out and unwrapped it and said, "Isn't she a beaut? That's real silver plating. Feel how easy she rests in your hand? Heavy, though, ain't it?" You nodded and said, "Big as a pork chop." Sykora thought that was funny. Green thought that was funny. No resemblance whatsoever. Sykora's wife said, eyes flitting at me as he noticed me opening the door, "There's a cop here now." A round fired. A spot appeared on her head. You were yanking your pistol from the holster when the next one hit. He shot only twice, her and you. You didn't even feel it—only pressure as you reeled back. Of course the warp of the windshield threw off his image, like shooting fish in a pond. But all those marksmanship trophies? Green kidded you about it in the hospital till he saw how it burned down inside.

Another car drove by blasting its horn. About five feet below the level of the road was a beam. It would be easy to get down there, Clay thought. Just to see how it feels. Nothing more. He waited for a car to pass, lest they think I am throwing myself in the river and call out the police or harbor patrol or Coast Guard to search for the body before it drifts too far. Floating (a man) facedown.

A truck passed and Clay waited, then climbed over the rail and lowered himself to the bar, reaching with the steel toe of his boot to find the surface and commit himself. He sat down, feeling the rumbling of vehicles up on the road. Steel rods planted in the beam stuck out another two feet over the river, and a cable was threaded through the eyes at the end. Clay clutched the cable. It was greasy. He thought, Greasy son of a bitch. What if you came in and found him with a gun? Does he own one? You should check at the sheriff's department; the permits are public record. No. Gordon is not Sykora. He might have hit her once, but he wouldn't. You liked him before they married. Before he hit her.

The cable was probably strong enough for him to hang from. Or someone else, Clay thought. Hang him from the bridge. Or maybe you should try it out—swing from it for a moment and then climb back up here. His heartbeat quickened, and he forbade himself to consider the idea. It was cold, and the gusts that followed the cars sent swirls of dirt and sand out from the bridge, and the grit glittered in the air and settled on his head and shoulders and the back of his neck like fine, icy snow. Clay's teeth chattered.

No sense of danger. Of course you knew what Kent was getting at. You should get out of here, out of this town, this job. What if you lose this job? Get out. There's a quick exit. Down to the river. Stop it. Get out of here.

Clay stood up. He climbed back on the bridge right in view of a car. His shadow startled him as it swept across the X-beam structure. Up here in the light the bolts on the steel resembled warts or some tumorous disease.

He walked back down the slope and compelled himself to stay on the sidewalk. Sometimes he came across pieces of plywood laid across the weak spots, and he stepped on each one. Grit stung his eyes. He glared at the headlights of each car that passed, and none of them honked. Cowards: willing to honk at a lonely back trudging up a bridge, but cowed by a man stomping down toward them holding their gaze. The road suddenly widened, and Clay was off the bridge, descending the ramp. He was overwhelmed with joy. He looked back. The bridge was already far away, and he began laughing aloud.

Sarah was not home when Clay arrived. Her bedroom door was open and her bed had not been slept in. She had spent several nights away from the house, but Clay had not commented on it when he saw her. The next morning was his day off, and he arose late and read the newspaper at the kitchen table while sipping a cup of coffee. Sarah came in through the back door. "Hi," she said. Clay glanced up and said, "Good morning." Her hair was still wet from her shower, and it hung in ringlets. "How was work last night?" she asked. "You were on graveyard, right?" Clay warmed the cup in his hands. "No, swing shift," he said. Then he told his sister what Kent had said, omitting the specific criticisms (walking under the crane) and making light of the whole thing. But Sarah was concerned.

"You shouldn't tell me that. It's so frightening. I wish you'd quit that job. Gordon said he saw you a couple of times at the mill but didn't say hi because he didn't want to distract you. You were threading paper through those blades that could slice a hand off, he said, or climbing up over the hydropulper."

"Nobody climbs above the hydropulper, so don't worry. I didn't mean to alarm you."

Sarah said, "At least if you found work elsewhere you could sleep at night like the rest of the higher mammals."

"Do you?"

"No, but I try."

She knelt and retied her shoelace. "Gordon just got switched to day shift."

"Good for him. When did he hear?"

"A couple of days ago."

Clay said, "I've actually been thinking of finding something else. I've got some money saved up, and I thought maybe I would do some traveling to the West Indies or the South Pacific. Maybe I could drive to Miami and get a job with the Immigration Service or the Coast Guard on one of those boats cruising the Caribbean."

"And end up as somebody's dinner."

Clay leaned forward, gesturing, and bumped his coffee cup, sloshing coffee out on the tablecloth. "Could be. But at least I won't tear myself to pieces in this town, or burn slowly for the next forty years working in a mill."

"Maybe you ought to find some ordinary job and take care of yourself for a while and let the scars heal."

"Oh, come on. I'm better." Clay noticed the coffee and began sopping it up with his napkin. "You should get away from here too. Ditch Gordon and go have an adventure."

Sarah leaned back on the sink and sighed. "Clay, there's something I need to tell you. Gordon and I are getting back together. Just for a short time, kind of a trial to see if it will be better now that he's working normal hours. And he's given up drinking. He hasn't had a drink in two weeks."

Clay slumped back and smacked his head on the wall. "Why? I don't understand why you would do that."

"I have to."

"You mean you choose to." Clay rubbed his eyes with his knuckles. "Aren't you afraid he'll kill you?" The words just slipped out. He regretted them.

Sarah came forward, clenching her fists, and said, "Jesus, would you get that out of your mind! You're obsessed with that. Gordon is not Sykora, okay? You have no idea what you're talking about. You're too caught up in your delusions."

She filled a cup with coffee from a pot on the stove and said, "I'm going back."

Night had fallen, and it was raining. Clay smelled the stink of the mills in the draft through the kitchen window, running his fingernail along the crack in the pane, thinking, Got to get this fixed. The steam from down by the river glowed beyond the wooden fence where a neighbor had spanked him with one of the slats he and a friend had broken off while playing in the yard. I was seven then. Dad marched over, red-faced, and threatened to use the stick on the neighbor, an old man who like father is now dead.

Clay chanted, "I'm gone now I'm gone now I'm gone," until he forgot the order and meaning of the words and said, "Stop it."

Something was cooking in the oven, and he grabbed a hot pad and opened the oven door to see what it was. When he lifted the lid of the dutch oven, steam blasted his wrist—he clattered the lid down and hopped around the room in agony, waving his hand. Then he turned on the cold water in the sink and stuck his wrist under the stream, but at once he thought, Now at last I have a burn on my wrist: perhaps it will scar: and that red patch the size of a silver dollar will remind me not to hope, not to think that two thousand dollars will buy adventure or justice or art (remember the architecture of the ceiling?), so he turned the water off and wrapped a towel around his wrist to burn the heat deep into it. He flexed his fingers, numb from the chill water.

He paced the room quickly in a narrowing circle, muttering, "Die, die, die, die, die," recalling by now not what his English teacher had said but simply that she had made an observation about the word, remembering the bones of the Orthodox saints, the vaults filled with skulls that had once been men (all of them men), painted and numbered in Greek, as if bone was more substantial than flesh, which melted away like a wax casting when the bronze is poured. His wrist hurt. He pressed his face to the windowpane and looked through the glass, which fogged an image like the face of the shroud. Then he paced the room in a constricting circle. He was dizzy.

"Stop it, Clay," he said.

In an act of will he sat down at the kitchen table. He prayed, "Christ, have mercy. Grant me thy peace."

Mrs. Breyssee came into the room and looked at the timer on the oven. Clay stood up and opened the back door.

"Where are you going?"

"I thought I'd grab a beer somewhere."

"You forgot your jacket." She took it from a hook by the door and slipped it on him.

"Thanks."

"Don't be long. We're eating in an hour."

"I won't."

Clay started out the door, and his mother touched his elbow.

"Are you all right, Clay?"

"Thanks. Yes, I'm fine. Thanks for asking."

He had forgotten his wallet, he realized when he reached the bar, and he had only a buck twenty-five in his pocket. He ordered a beer at the bar and shot a game of pool with an unemployed carpenter. Then he moved to a table in the corner, where he could watch the room. His wrist throbbed. Sandy was on duty, and she came over to his table.

"Hi, Clay. You want another beer?"

"No, thanks. This is fine."

"What happened to your wrist?"

"I burned it checking something in the oven."

"Ouch. That must hurt."

"Not really."

She leaned over and took his hand as if reading his palm. "It looks like it's starting to blister. Want me to get some ice?"

"No, that's all right. I'm holding it against my beer to cool it."

"Well, that beer won't cool it much. You've been nursing it for the past half hour. It must be room temperature by now. Let me bring you another."

"No, thank you."

"Come on. On the house. Just don't tell the boss."

"Well, all right. Thanks, that sounds good." He finished the old beer.

Sandy went to the bar and drew a beer, pumping with her thin arm like an African woman at the village tap. Then she came and set the schooner in front of Clay.

"Hold it against your wrist," she said.

His wrist ached against the cold glass.

"May I join you?" she said, sitting down before he could respond. He would have said yes. Their reflections were harsh and stark on the dark window beside the table. Outside a neon shamrock was flickering.

"What are you up to these days?" Sandy asked.

"I'm thinking about going to the West Indies."

"No kidding! When?"

"I don't know. Pretty soon, I imagine."

"Wow, that's really exciting. What are you going to do there?"

"Find some job. Travel. I just want to see what it's like there."

"Take me in your suitcase when you go. Jeez, I've always wanted to travel and just lie out on some beach and have somebody wait on me. That's the impression I've always had of the West Indies. Kerri says I should get a job as a travel agent."

Clay sipped his beer.

Sandy said, "Didn't that guy who was in here the other night—the fat guy—you remember who I mean? Carson. Didn't Carson say his best friend used to live in the West Indies?"

"Somewhere like that, I think."

Sandy pressed his wrist against the schooner again, then glanced at the coffee machine behind the bar. "What a lucky guy," she said.

Pictures of Her Snake

In retrospect, Julie saw that her relationship with Sean had been ailing months before the anaconda appeared in her house; the end had been in sight as long ago as the night he hopped around on the furniture in his boxer shorts, bellowing lines from *Look Back in Anger,* and tried to hit her with a bottle of Cutty Sark. But after he photographed the snake, everything collapsed. Sean promised never to show the pictures to anyone, but he said he needed to develop them in the darkroom of the weekly newspaper where he worked. Someone found the contact sheets and showed them around the newsroom, and the metro editor persuaded Sean to let him run one of the photos. A reporter phoned Julie at the office to interview her for an article that would accompany the picture; she resisted talking at first and threatened to sue if it ran but finally spilled out the entire story, concluding, "You hear about this kind of thing happening in Calcutta and places like that—but in Seattle, in Magnolia?"

The comment looked silly in print, and a minister who ran a rescue mission on skid row wrote the paper in response: "The poor and destitute of this community would be delighted to exchange their newspapers and park benches for a home in Magnolia, even one in which a reptile was known to appear in the commode." The next week a professor of women's studies at the University of Washington wrote another letter, objecting to a biblical allusion the minister had made: in the original myth, she said, the snake had been Eve's lesbian lover, and together they had begotten the world and humankind. In both cases the paper reprinted a smaller version of Sean's photograph. Then Julie overheard a senior attorney at the office explaining that he had clipped the original article, the letters, and all the pictures and posted them inside the door of the men's room stall. He giggled, "And was it you who drew the tattoo on her thigh?" "Shhh," another voice said, "I think she's sitting right out there in the other room." That evening she asked Sean to leave.

The worst thing was that Julie had no idea how long the

snake had been around. It was the sort of thing she could imagine one of Sean's friends sneaking into the house as a joke, and though he became enraged when she said this and nearly tore the print he was removing from the wall (a surrealistic lithograph of a limp, drooping Space Needle), she could name at least one precedent: the time Bart left the hand of a baboon he had dissected in a tray of developing solution in Sean's darkroom. She refused to entertain the notion that the snake might have slithered all the way up the plumbing from the sewers; when Sean suggested this, she crossed her legs and shuddered in horror.

The morning it happened, Sean was eating Wheaties in the breakfast nook and writing a funny caption under the photograph on the front of the box, a picture of an Olympic star drooling milk as she ate her cereal. Julie screamed in the bathroom. Sean later told the reporter he thought he had left the toilet seat up and she had sat down on the porcelain rim. But she kept yelling, and he flew down the hall to investigate. Julie, dressed in her bathrobe, flung open the door and shrieked, "Sean! Look at that thing!" She clenched her fists, and as he touched her arm to get past her he felt her trembling.

"What?"

"Look!" She pointed at the toilet. Sean stepped closer and made a face as he peered in. A slick green object like the intestine of a cow was looped around the bowl, and both ends disappeared in a mush of paper. He shrugged and observed, "Why, that has got to be the largest turd I've ever seen."

"It's a snake!" said Julie, purple with rage.

"A snake?"

"Yes."

"Where did it come from?"

"I didn't put it there, that's for sure. I just heard this sloshing in the water, and I got up to look and there it was. I'm glad it didn't try to bite me, or I'd be dead now."

Sean said, "I imagine it's seen more appetizing sights in its life."

Julie threw her hairdryer at him. He ducked, and it clattered against the mirror and broke on the floor. The snake writhed and splashed water on the carpet.

"Wait, I was only kidding," he said. He stood and stared at the bowl. "That's incredible. Hold on just one second," he told the snake. Sean ran from the room.

By the time he returned with his camera, Julie had fetched a hoe from the garden and was tugging on the snake's body.

"Great," said Sean, and he began shooting pictures.

"Would you put your damn camera aside and lend me a hand?" she said.

"Okay. One second. Hang on. Can you lift it a little higher? Good. Perfect." Sean took the camera from around his neck and set it on the sink. "All right, now give me that hoe. I'll take care of it."

He tugged on the handle, but the snake was wedged tight and refused to budge. Sean turned around and tugged with his foot against the toilet, but he slipped and nearly fell back through the open shower door. He rested for a moment.

"How on earth did it get jammed in there so tight?" he mused.

Julie said, "I'll try flushing the toilet while you pull."

She pushed the handle with her thumb, and water swirled to the rim and lapped onto the floor.

"It's starting to come free," said Sean.

"Which end is coming first?"

He eased his grip and looked at her, wiping his brow. "Maybe you should get the ax."

"Ax?"

"So we can chop its head off when it comes out."

A moment later Julie returned with a rusty ax with a nicked and dirty haft. She braced herself, feet spread, and raised the ax over her head. The blade bumped the ceiling, and flakes of plaster speckled her hair.

Sean said, "What are you doing? You'll lop my head off."

Julie lowered the ax. "I wanted to be ready."

"Flush again," said Sean. He pulled the snake a few inches further, and a faint popping sound came from the toilet.

"What's that?" asked Julie.

"It feels like its back is dislocating."

"Oh, that's dreadful."

"Flush again."

Perspiration dripped from Sean's face to the floor. He grunted and tugged. The snake writhed weakly. Sean shifted his weight, positioning one foot against the toilet rim, and pulled on the snake with a groan. "It's coming," he gasped. The tail whipped free, and Sean fell backward through the open shower doorway.

"Grab it!" he shouted. "Don't let it get away."

Julie snatched up the snake's tail. "Sean—" she said, her voice rising in horror. The snake's skin was soft, and its muscles worked in her hands. "Sean, would you get off your butt and help me!"

This was the moment she later recognized as the dividing line in her relationship with Sean: he leapt to his feet and snatched his camera from the sink. "Just a sec," he said and started shooting. One shot in particular proved fatal to what she had once thought was love for him: a picture of her arms and hands (her nails long, filed sharp, painted) as she grasped the tail of an anaconda that stretched four feet from the toilet bowl; her bathrobe obligingly parted, and a shapely leg entered one side of the picture. From all you could tell in the photograph, she might have been nude.

Julie said, "Put that down and give me a hand, you idiot."

"Right. Gotcha. Good. This, yes, this is all I need." He set his camera aside, and together they pulled the limp reptile onto the wet floor. The snake was at least fifteen feet long.

"Kill it," said Sean. "Chop its head off."

The snake twitched on the bathroom floor, hissing. Sean snatched the ax. "If you won't, I will." He hacked at the snake, gashing it in several spots. But his aim was bad, and he also

splintered the cabinet beneath the sink and gouged the linoleum and the carpet. The snake looped itself slowly, hissing in
agony. It smeared blood across the floor.

Julie said, "Don't. Wait a second."

Sean leaned on the ax like a cane, breathing heavily. "For
Pete's sake, I thought you wanted to kill it."

"Maybe we can call the zoo or a vet or something."

"Julie, there's no way that thing will live. Look at it: its back
is broken."

"Well, take it outside before you chop my bathroom to
pieces. Look at that blood everywhere. How am I supposed to
clean that up?"

Sean picked the snake up with the hoe and dragged it out
to the backyard, its intestines bulging through a gash on its
side. He flopped it in the dirt beside the woodpile and ran
back for his camera. Julie knelt in the bathroom, wiping the
floor with a towel.

"Did you kill it?"

"I forgot the ax."

Sean grabbed the ax and his camera and ran back through
the house. As he rounded the chopping block in the kitchen,
he slipped in a puddle of blood and knocked his bowl of soggy
Wheaties to the floor. He trotted outside. Adam, the neighbor's dalmatian, had squeezed through a gap where a board
was missing in the fence, and he yelped and wagged his tail
and sniffed the snake's wounds and hissing mouth. Sean fo-
cused his camera, set the shutter speed, and began shooting.

The back door boomed open against the side of the house,
and Julie bounded down the stairs with her robe open on her
naked body, the blood-spattered cloth flowing behind from
the cord around her waist. "Get away!" she shouted at Adam.
"Go on. Get." She snatched up the ax Sean had left standing
against the woodpile and chased off the dog, which yipped
and buried his tail between his haunches and fled down the
alley. Julie returned to the serpent and raised the ax and

brought down the blade. She severed the snake's head and sliced deep in the turf. The head snapped blindly.

She turned, panting, to Sean. He grinned and replaced the cap on his lens.

"That was great," he said, picking a hair from his tongue.

Julie chased him twice around the house with the ax, trampling the petunias in the flower beds, before he managed to convince her he was only kidding.

The Monkey

During summer in the desert the snow stayed late on the mountains, telescoped in the swirling pellucid air, and the wash was filled with a clear cold stream that formed a deep pool where we could swim naked and where Titus almost drowned. That was our first summer in the desert and our hottest. "Stay in the shade," Mom told Titus when he followed us. Ted yelled, "Mom says you can't come with us! You have to stay in the yard." I squinted. Our shadows were small around our feet. Mom was standing in the doorway saying, "Nobody's going to be the odd man out. Besides, I don't want any of you playing in the sun."

"Can't Titus stay home?" I asked. "He's the guy who gets hot." Titus came following and said, "I want to go with you guys."

"You're not going to go trekking into the Mojave in the heat of the day. I want all of you to stay wthin hollering distance—and out of the sun."

The heat shimmered on the ground and filled the dry washes and lake beds with mirages that made your mouth water, and it painted false dark stripes of moisture across either end of the street where we lived, as if a hose had been left running, but the stripes evaporated as you ran toward them. The asphalt was soft and clung in sticky pellets to your shoes. Before entering the house, we had to remove our shoes in the screened-in porch—still filled with boxes from our last move—where Wolfgang the cat had unexpectedly borne a litter of kittens that spring. Dad also found a rattler on the porch once. We looked up at the San Gabriel Mountains from the desert floor as we excavated an abandoned coyote den under a creosote bush near our house; and when you stepped out of our cool dark stucco manse at midday, the white snowcaps and hot desert floor and cobalt blue sky blinded you. "The hot white air," said Teddy. I shut my eyes. The light was unbearable.

Then Mrs. Neukom's husband visited her, and we heard

shouting and cusswords at night, and Mom said, "I can call the sheriff just in case." Then Dad said something in the hall. He passed the door of our room, leaning forward as he walked, and the front door shut. "What's going on?" said Titus sleepily. I said, "I think Dad's going to get in a fight." Titus stirred. "Who with?" he asked. I tried looking out the window, but it faced the wrong way, out onto the blue moonlit desert. The moon was waning, and a perfect nimbus surrounded it. "I don't know," I said, "someone at Mrs. Neukom's house." Titus said, "Is he big—the guy Dad's fighting?" I lay back in bed and told him, "I don't know. I don't even know if Dad's really going to fight." A coyote howled. It was quiet across the street. "I'm scared," Titus said. "Shhh," I said, "let's listen." There was more shouting, and a car door slammed. When Dad came back I called to him in the hallway, "Where were you, Dad?" He came to the door. "You boys ought to be asleep now," he said. "I was praying with Mrs. Neukom and her husband. Now he's gone."

"Did you get in a fight?" Titus asked.

"Of course not." Dad tucked us in.

"Andy said you were going to get in a fight."

"No, I didn't, I said maybe he was going to get in a fight."

"Well, Andy was wrong. Now go to sleep."

I sat up in bed. "I didn't know she had a husband."

"Lie down. She does, but he left town. He just drove away. No more questions. Go to sleep."

We closed our eyes, and Dad went away.

The next morning it rained lightly, pattering the sand and covering it with pockmarks, and even after the rain passed and the sky began to clear, Mom kept us inside because she was afraid of flash floods. But then she decided we were getting too rambunctious, and she shooed us outdoors. Across the street, Mrs. Neukom had a spider monkey in a cage in her front yard. One of the old lady's eyes was puffy and red. She said, "That's the only thing Mr. Neukom ever gave me, boys: a stinking monkey. What the hell am I supposed to do with that?"

For a while we no longer played near the coyote den, catching scorpions and feeding them to the swarms of red-and-black ants in the conical anthills. Ted unlatched the door to the cage and crawled in with the monkey, and he got in trouble when Titus told. We named the monkey Judas because Mrs. Neukom said her husband who gave it to her was a traitor. She was unaware that Ted was crouching in the cage, scratching the monkey, which she had told us not to touch, behind the ears: she napped in the afternoon, and she did not care if we played with Judas under the shade of the poplars as long as we were quiet and let her sleep. The Mormon boys Ralf and Roger said their mother forbade them to enter Mrs. Neukom's yard because the old lady got to sleep by drinking from a bottle of rum. Ted said only pirates drank rum, but Mrs. Neukom was drinking something. Once we woke her, and we were afraid, but she came out and sat in the dirt with her ankles crossed, pulling her skirt down over her knees, and crooned to Judas. "Isn't he a ratty little beast?" she said. She went back into her house. That only happened once. Ralf and Roger hung on the gate and watched us speak softly to Judas. Roger had a stammer.

Ted rubbed Judas on the belly. You could see the monkey's nipples through his sparse hair. I said, "Don't touch him. Mom says he's filthy." Ted kept scratching Judas, and he said, "Look, Judas has a belly button."

"Where?"

"Right there. See?"

"Get out of the cage before Mom sees you."

The cage reeked of the monkey's dirty pelt and his green-black feces, spotted with white seeds from the oranges he ate. Mrs. Neukom let us feed him. He accepted orange sections in his tiny, black-gloved hand, turning over and examining each piece, then raising his eyebrows and biting it.

"Feed Ted an orange," I said. "Ted is a monkey."

"Shut up."

Titus said, "I'm telling Mom you said 'shut up.'"

"There, you said it too."

"Ted is a monkey," said Titus.

Ted fumbled at the latch and said, "I'm going to come out there and hit you."

"Teddy is a monkey," Titus said. He chanted, "Monkey, monkey, Moonbeam the monkey."

"Look what you started," Ted told me.

"Okay, Titus," I said.

"Monkey," Titus said, and he laughed.

Sometimes Judas started when we came near and fled to the back of his cage, and we would coax him in small voices until he chattered and came forward and looked at us. "He has probably been mistreated," Mom said. Mrs. Neukom set the cage too close to the cholla cactus, trying to keep it in the shade of the house when she went to the store to buy Judas canned dog food, and he reached through the chicken wire and grabbed the cactus. The monkey was screaming and jumping about in his cage when we found him. He bit at his fingers till his hands bled. Mrs. Neukom pulled the spines out with tweezers, but she said she couldn't afford to take him to the veterinarian. "I don't have the money to throw away on a dying monkey," she said. "I didn't want him in the first place. If you want Judas you can have him. Tell your parents to take him to the vet." But Mom and Dad refused to keep a pet monkey. "When Dad graduates we'll probably find a church in the city," Mom said. "We can't cart a monkey around with us when we look for an apartment." Judas did not eat the dog food, and Mrs. Neukom gave us the rest. We fed it to Wolfgang.

I said, "I wonder if Judas is really dying."

"Of course not," Ted insisted. He was lying on his belly in the sparse brown grass. "Mrs. Neukom just hates animals."

Titus said, "He looks sick."

"So does Roger, but he's not dying."

"What?" Roger called over the gate, and we laughed.

Titus said, "Give him some m&m's. I'm going to give him some m&m's."

Once Mrs. Neukom stuffed some stale raspberry fruit leather in the cage, then told us never to give Judas candy. "These are different," she said. "They're made out of fruit. And only I can give them." We let Titus feed the monkey. Titus pulled the wadded candy package from his pocket and gave a few to Judas.

Ted said, "I'm telling. You'll make Judas' teeth fall out."

Titus said, "I'll tell you got in the cage."

"I haven't done that since you told last week. You can't tell on something twice. You're just trying to stop me so you won't get in trouble for trying to make Judas' teeth rot."

Titus cried.

Ted said, "Promise you'll stop annoying?"

"I promise."

"Maybe I'll tell anyway. You deserve it for annoying us."

"Teddy!" Titus' eyes and cheeks were puffy and red.

"He won't tell," I said. "He said he wouldn't as long as you promise not to annoy."

"I promise."

But when Titus got home he told on himself.

Titus staggered back from the desert gnashing a mouthful of sand. His eye sockets were smudged with dirty shadows, and a piece of cholla was jabbed into his brow. His face was blood-caked in dried rivulets, and his Maranatha T-shirt was stained and torn where he had thrashed in the sand. A spine from a Joshua tree was embedded in the muscle of his calf. My leg throbbed: it made your flesh ache to even prick your-self on a Joshua spine. "What happened, Titus?" I said, and my eyes felt tight. I was always like that afterward when I saw Titus, but I knew how to hold it back so nothing would happen. He could not have wandered very far into the desert, but he looked as if he had returned from a distance, from the Lovejoy Buttes or even the Low Desert and the abandoned mines in the treeless hills around Calico and Johannesburg and Hierosolyma, where there was a mine shaft dropping straight down that was dotted every fifteen feet with lights. The shaft was covered with wire mesh. There were torn spots in the mesh, and you could drop pennies through the holes, and the bits of copper disappeared soundlessly or pinged against the void and continued falling. Dad swatted you and said, "Stop that. There might be someone down there," and then he leaned over and peered into the void and said, "How would you like to be a miner descending in that rickety elevator every day?" Titus would not look in the shaft, and you imagined he had seen something down there, staring—as Grandma said, who never in her life swore or took the Lord's name in vain—into the gates of hell. At least he came limping home now.

I ran to Titus, pulled the piece of cholla from his face, and he said, "Ow." I thought, At least he is feeling. I put my arm around his shoulders. His shirt was dry. Titus never sweats. "How are you doing, buddy?" I asked. "It's okay. Hey, Titus." Titus made a noise and tried to shrug me away. He drooled a long gleaming thread. It was too early for him to talk. He was flushed and near sunstroke.

"Here, lean on me, buddy. Come on, Titus. That's right."

His muscles were still stiff and powerful, and he had not begun to relax yet. When it happened you saw his pupils dilate and his eyes stare like Grandma said. I was afraid to pull the barb out; its edges were serrated so they caught and tore the flesh. We walked toward the house. Titus leaned heavily on me. He limped.

"There's the house, Titus," I said. He stumbled on a rock. "Whoa. Watch it. Look, it's nice and cool up there. How are you doing? That-a-boy."

Titus spoke.

"What?" I said. "Let's keep going. We're almost there."

He halted and bent over.

"No, buddy. Let Mom do that up at the house. See the house? It's shady and cool there."

Titus sat or collapsed beside a juniper. The sun was hot on the back of my neck. I was afraid of scorpions and rattlesnakes by the base of the tree.

Titus worked the spine back and forth. Big tears ran down his cheeks, and my eyes tightened.

"You're only hurting yourself. Hey, Titus, will you stop it?"

He pulled on the barb, but it would not break off.

"Wait. Here, let me do it. Come on."

I grabbed the spine and yanked it from his flesh. It tore the muscle, and he cried out. It was a foot long, and half of it had been buried in his leg. I tasted blood.

"Let's go, Titus."

Titus rubbed his calf and smeared the blood. He stood up. His face was purple now. He opened his mouth. Then he began stumbling toward the cluster of houses across the street, where Mrs. Neukom lived.

"No, this way, Titus. We're almost home."

He moaned and struggled.

Ted saw us and ran over to help restrain Titus. He said, "How did his leg get all bloody?" and then hollered, "Mom!"

"Titus," I said.

"Why is he trying to head over there? Does he want to see the monkey or something?"

"He doesn't know what he wants," I said. "Mom!"

We fell down with Titus on top of us, and we were laughing but we stopped ourselves.

"He had one of those Joshua tree stabbers in his leg. I pulled it out."

"He's all bloody," Ted said admiringly.

"Let's get him on his feet."

Mom came rushing out and helped us stand Titus up.

Titus was sleeping in the bedroom with a cold washcloth on his forehead. It was dinnertime, and we begged Mom and Dad to buy us the monkey.

"Mrs. Neukom said she'd sell him to us for forty dollars," Ted said.

"The price has gone up," Dad observed. "I seem to recall that last week he was free."

"She found out he's very valuable," I said. "He's worth a thousand dollars."

"The answer is no," Mom said. "You never know what terrible diseases that animal might have. And I don't want you boys touching him."

"He's not diseased. He's a clean monkey."

"I don't think he would get along with Wolfgang."

"Yes, he would," Ted said. "Judas likes cats."

Dad said, "You boys have had your answer. The next person who says anything about a monkey is going straight to bed without dessert."

"Aw, Dad," said Ted.

"I mean it."

Under the table Ted spelled out M-O-N-K-E-Y on my leg. I said, "Ted, quit monkeying around." We laughed. Dad sent me to bed.

It was evening, and the light was no longer white but golden on the sandy ground between the creosotes and yuccas and Joshua trees that I could see from my window. The sun took a long time to set. Ted came in with something wrapped in a paper napkin. "It's a cookie," he said. "I swiped one for Titus too." He glanced dubiously at Titus and said, "You might as well eat it." I said, "Thanks," and Teddy left. I plugged in my night-light under the window. As twilight came, strange desert insects collected on the screen: black widow spiders and beetles and vinegarroons and spotted moths whose paper wings trembled in the exchange of air between the bedroom and the night. Once I tapped on the screen and sent the insects flying, but they returned. Titus was quietly breathing in his bed. The washcloth had slipped from his forehead: it was bunched beside his ear and formed a damp spot on his pillow. After dark Mom and Dad entered our room. They kissed me, and I pretended to be asleep. Dad's whiskers scoured my cheek. They whispered beside Titus' bed. Dad said, "We ought to get him to a real doctor, not one of these semiretired hicks who move out to California for the sun and cheap property."

"We should."

They were quiet for a moment. Dad put his arm around her.

"It will be expensive," Mom said.

"Maybe we're eligible for state assistance or something, given the stipend the church pays."

"Why don't you check that out in Pasadena? Or I can go over with you some day this week and look into it and make an appointment with a doctor over there."

"Maybe. Yes, that's a good idea."

Mom sat on the bed. Dad said sotto voce, "I've got to go study." He kissed the top of her head, and she looked up and he kissed her lips. She patted his leg. Then Dad ambled out the door and down the creaking hallway. Mom ran her fingers through Titus' fine black hair. He moaned, and she made a slight noise and kissed him. She came over to my bed and bent down and kissed me. Her face was hot and wet. She said, "Good night, perfect boy." She went away. For a long time I lay in bed and looked at the insects swirling upside down on the screen, their legs like wisps of gold thread against the night, and I felt empty inside.

The stream rushed over the rocks and into the pool, and Teddy and I would sneak up to the water hole and strip and leap off the bank into the water. Ralf and Roger came across us once when they were hunting for arrowheads, and Ralf said, "Hey, look at the faggots; they're naked," but Ted jumped out of the water and chased Ralf up the wash with a stick while Roger screamed. They came back, and we persuaded Ralf to swim, though he would not remove his cutoffs. Roger sat on the embankment and watched. "You're going to get it when you get home, Ralf," he said. Ralf said, "Mom won't know unless you fink." He tried to splash Roger, but Roger moved away. Roger made a face, as he did when he had trouble saying a word. "She'll see your shorts are wet." Ralf said, "They'll dry." Then he asked me, "What's wrong with your brother?" I said, "What's wrong with your face?" Ralf said, "I was just asking." By midsummer the stream had soaked into the sand and left a string of diminishing pools and mud puddles. The water warmed and grew sluggish, and moss grew as it did on the surface of Mrs. Neukom's swimming pool. But now it was still clear, and Dad said, "I can't believe we didn't see him right away; the water was like glass." We ate cold chicken first at the house, and Mom made us wait an hour before we swam. We all sat at the kitchen table in our swimsuits.

"Can we go now?" I said.

"It's only been a minute since you asked the last time," Mom said.

"Why don't you boys go hunt for lizards?" Dad suggested.

"Can we play with Judas?" Titus said.

"If Mrs. Neukom doesn't mind."

Judas was breathing feverishly in the heat. Mrs. Neukom came out in her slippers and gave each of us a candy bar. We thanked her. "Don't tell those Kennedy boys," she said, "that's all I have." Judas drank from his plastic cup of water. I said, "I think Judas is sick."

Mrs. Neukom bent over and said, "Do you want me to take your candy bar away? Do you? Because I've had about all I'm willing to put up with about Judas' health. It would take about six years of your allowance to pay for one visit to the vet. Do you want to cover that? Do you want to ask your dad for a six-year advance on your allowance?"

"No, ma'am."

"Well, then don't nag me about it. Do you understand?"

"Yes."

"I don't know why I bother to buy you boys treats. I could be putting that toward Judas' medical treatment. Do you think that would be better? Do you?"

I got up and set my candy bar on Judas' cage. Judas looked up and blinked; then he stood on his hind feet and poked at the candy from beneath and tried to get his fingers around it.

"Now don't do that," Mrs. Neukom said. "I'm not asking you to do that. I bought it for you. I just want you boys to think about what this all means to me."

"No, thanks."

I left. Ted and Titus kept their candy bars, and by the time we got to the house I was wondering if it was too late to run back and snatch mine from the top of the cage.

"Let's go," said Dad.

The bank was steep and gravelly, and cottonwoods shaded the pool in the afternoon. The water came rushing down from the rocks, and downstream it went around a bend. Titus dug a channel along the shore for the boat he had made in Cub Scouts. Ted shouted, "Mom and Dad, look!" and took a deep breath and submerged, and he swam the length of the pool without coming up to breathe, passing swiftly and frantically under Dad, like a slick manatee in an aquarium, while Dad floated in an innertube and read the *Los Angeles Times* Sunday Opinion section. Ted emerged gasping.

"Good job," Dad said too soon for him to hear.

"You didn't even look," Ted brayed.

"Yes, I did. I saw you. Good job."

I clenched my hands together and swept them back and forth, splashing up on the bank, and the water ran back in muddy rivulets. Ted said, "What are you doing?"

"Watering the desert."

"Don't get the water up here," Titus said. "I'm digging a harbor."

Ted also began splashing. "Look, Mom, we're making a tidal wave." Mom sat on the opposite bank, leaning against a tree and reading a book. She wore the straw hat Dad had bought her in Mexico. "Good," she said.

"Hey, watch it," Dad said. "You're getting my paper all wet."

"Gang up on Dad," I said.

"Okay, hang on a second. Let me get rid of my paper."

Dad hoisted himself out of his innertube and waded to the shore. He tossed the section up the bank to Mom, and she snatched it and tucked it into a cloth handbag at her feet.

We splashed Dad, and a hot dry gust from the gully scudded the spray across the bank. "Titus, gang up on Dad," I said. Dad waded forward, shielding his eyes with his hand turned palm outward, and he grabbed Ted and tossed him squealing into the center of the pool. Ted came up splashing in the wrong direction before his eyes cleared and he sprayed Dad in the face with a jet of water. "Where's Titus?" Mom said. Dad grabbed me and flung me across the pool. I went in the water and heard a boiling noise as I exhaled, and I came up and splashed in sweeping motions. Dad said something. I splashed toward the sound of his voice. He grabbed me in his arms, and I struggled against his hairy wet chest. "Andy!" he said. "Stop it, Andy. Look for Titus."

"What?"

"Titus is missing. Search the pool."

He released me, and I wiped the water from my face and began walking upstream slowly, bent double. A tab from a beer can gleamed between two rocks.

Dad reached into the water and pulled a foot from the glaring surface. He scrambled halfway up the bank, dragging Titus by the armpits. He bent Titus over his knee and worked his arms, and Titus coughed up a yellow fluid. Dad turned him over and gave him mouth-to-mouth resuscitation. Ted and I watched shivering from the pool. The water was cold. Titus coughed.

Mom said, "Get up here, boys. Put your shoes on."

We dashed up the bank. I stubbed my toe and slid back, and gravel and hot sand scalded between my toes. Mom gave Ted the car key. "Get over to the house and start the car."

Dad appeared over the bank carrying Titus, and Mom knelt and jammed his high-top basketball shoes on his feet. "What?" he said.

"You can't charge back there barefoot."

Ted and I ran back with the hot air billowing in our lungs. We heard Dad and Mom lumbering through the sage behind us. Ted got to start the car.

Dad drove with Titus in front between him and Mom. Titus breathed shallowly and sometimes choked. "Put his head between his knees where he won't gag," Dad said. Titus' head hit the dashboard. The speedometer read ninety miles an hour past Eddie Eckhardt's house and the sign that said, "Buy an Acre of California Sun." When we got to the irrigated lowlands, the air through the vents and windows got cooler and humid and smelled like hay.

Mom glanced back over her shoulder and said, "You boys don't have your seat belts on. Fasten them right now." Her straw hat brushed her shoulder strap.

Dad asked, "How's he doing? Breathing okay?"

"Yes. Not great, though."

Mom pulled Titus' head over on her lap and breathed in his mouth, puffing his cheeks. The sun glared through the windshield, and the light through her hat cast a latticework of shadows on their faces. He groaned and writhed weakly. Mom stopped.

A man in white accepted Titus, head flopping back, from Dad's arms, and he padded down the hallway with Dad fol-

lowing. Lights in square ceiling panels cast a bright incandes-
cence and traced a faint blue line around the man's white
coat and trousers. The lights were buzzing. Mom said, "Wait
here on this bench, boys." A nurse standing there with her
hands on her hips said, "Before you take off after your son
we'd better take a look at those feet." Mom was barefoot, and
her feet were bloody and bruised and pierced with cactus
spines in thin yellow lumps under the skin. I said, "Does
it hurt?" Mom said with her face stiffening, "You boys wait quietly here," and followed the nurse into a room, smearing
bloody footprints on the linoleum, while Ted and I sat swinging our feet.

Dad said the doctor used an electric shock to make Titus
have a seizure: "Like a cattleprod to make the poor dumb animal go the way you want it to," he said at dinner, "prodding a
steer up the right chute to the slaughterhouse." "Alan," said
Mom. Mom told the doctor, "We already know that." Dad
said, trembling with rage, "We just took him to a specialist in
Pasadena last week. A neurologist." The doctor insisted, "Yes,
but don't you see? He must have had a seizure while he was
swimming." He stifled a smile at the discovery he had made.
Dad said, "We already know that." The doctor raised his hand
patiently, "This of course can be treated in most cases with
medication. Three or four little capsules a day will take care
of this sort of thing in ninety percent of the cases. He can lead
a normal life. Maybe even go swimming without being afraid
of going under and nobody seeing him." Dad said, "He's been
on medication for two years." The doctor looked annoyed
and puzzled. Dad said, "Boys, would you please wait outside?"
Titus was asleep. We left. "What if what they're saying goes
into his dreams?" I said. Ted slugged me lightly and said, "It
won't. You can't hear when you're asleep."
    "It's true," Dad said. "It's completely senseless. He seems to
be trying to demonstrate empirically the validity of every-

thing he learned in med school on the subject of epilepsy. He's using our son as a guinea pig. And keeping Titus in the hospital for four days: that's outrageous."

"Why did he shock Titus?" Ted asked.

"That's what we don't understand," Mom said.

"Was it a metal stick that he held like a cattleprod?" Dad said, "No, it was a machine plugged into the wall." He looked at Mom and raised his eyebrows. "Maybe we'd better change the subject."

"I think so."

"We ought to pray for the doctor," I said.

Dad looked at me for a moment. "Come here, Andy," he said. He sat me on his lap and hugged me and bowed his head, nose and lips on my scalp, breath tickling my cowlick. We sat for a long time in silence before Mom began to pray.

Titus no longer wore the hospital gown with a slit down the back; he wore regular cutoffs and tennis shoes, and he went outside the first morning and caught ants on a stick, probing deep into the anthills and withdrawing it swarming with ants, which he shook off into a soft-drink can. He urinated in the can and shook it up to make ant stew. "You're gross," said Ted. Titus laughed. "We can feed it to the monkey," he said. He raised the can as if in a toast. "Don't be cruel," I said. Ted said, "I wonder if Judas would drink it." I snatched the can from Titus and dumped it out. "You guys are sick," I said. Titus laughed and then said, "How is the monkey? I want to see Judas."

It was hot and dusty, and the sky was dun with a rare smog that drifted in from the other side of the mountains. You could not see the buttes. The wind rattled in the dry leafy poplars and swept tumbleweeds along the sand and collected them in a shifting mass on the sides of ditches. Sometimes a tumbleweed in a ditch leapt free from the others and scuttled out across the desert. Mom said we could go to Mrs. Neukom's.

The monkey's cage was not in front of the house.

"Maybe she moved him in back since we weren't around to play with him," Ted mused.

We knocked on the peeling wooden frame of the front screen, rattling it against the door. Through the flimsy curtain I saw someone moving around. Mrs. Neukom opened the door and looked through the screen. Her face was puffy and red. She said, "If it's the monkey you want, he's not here any longer."

"What happened to him? Where is he?"

"Christ, I don't know. Where do monkeys go? You boys ought to know."

"What do you mean?"

"He was a very sick animal, Titus. He had to be put to sleep. Isn't Mrs. Neukom evil, boys? Maybe I'll go to hell; that's what you think, isn't it? You had me figured all along, didn't you?"

Ted said in a high voice, "Why did you do that?"

"He was sick, too sick to live. The monkey was suffering. You don't care about that, do you? You boys just wanted a toy. I tried to save him, but he was dying. Now get. You won't have any reason to come see Mrs. Neukom now."

Mom said we could walk down to the store if Titus wore a hat to keep the sun off his face, and Ted and I decided to raid Mrs. Neukom's on the way. "She could've at least tried to get him some medicine or treatment or something," I said. Titus lagged behind. "What if we get in trouble?" he asked. Ted flipped the brim of Titus' cowboy hat and said, "You don't have to come with us." Titus followed us. We crept on our bellies through the sage and told ourselves we were Dakotas avenging the death of a member of our tribe, our medicine man whose symbol was the moon, who had fallen in battle with the white eyes. We would count many coups. We would destroy the white eyes. We heard a shuffling noise. Titus was standing behind us in his shorts and hat and oversize cowboy boots. "Get down!" Ted hissed. Titus stopped. He sucked on his finger and watched us crawl on. "Make him get down," I told Ted. Ted said, "Shhh!"

We came up to Mrs. Neukom's chain-link fence. Her pool was stagnant and murky, with moss growing on the surface, and we began lobbing dirt clods into the water. The clods parted the moss and splashed it out on the tile and concrete. We whispered our war cry lest we rouse their sentries: "Hoka hey." The hated white eyes. The hated Mrs. Neukom, the murderer. Then the door swung open, and Mrs. Neukom came out. Her hair was tangled, and she was dressed in a slip and a man's flowered print shirt. She stumbled on the step and fell on the concrete. We were too frightened to flee. She screamed, "Go away! Stop it, you little wretches. I took him to a vet, can't you understand? Judas was sick, and the vet said he had to put him to sleep. Come over here right now. I'm going to march you straight to your mother. Come here." We ran in terror.

We boomed through the screen door of the Pearblossom Shopper and almost upset the fan that clattered away on a chair beside the coffee machine, which was unplugged all summer, with a brown crust cooked to the bottom of the pot. Mr. Burroughs said, "Whoa now. Slow down." We bought some gum, and Titus caught up and found us hiding behind the rack reading comics, and we chewed gum and gave him some and stayed there memorizing Batman comics (the slant of his ears, the shape of the emblem on his square chest, the lines on his abdomen) so we could draw them when we got home, until Mr. Burroughs came back and snatched them from our hands and said, "Look at these. Just look at them. They're all smudged. Buy it or beat it." We filed out through the door with the bell dinging, and he told a fat woman buying potato chips and powdered milk with food stamps: "They're too poor to buy the damn comics, so instead they come in and thumb them to pieces. Their dad is the Methodist minister. Doesn't it figure? Preacher's kids are always the worst."

On the way back up the long dusty road Ted said, "Titus, you'd better not tell on us for throwing things in Mrs. Neukom's pool or we'll get you. I mean that"; and I added, "Or for smudging the comics." There was a flash of sun on chrome half a mile up the road by our street, and Ted said, "Car." I said, "I think it's Mrs. Neukom's Dodge. I think she's looking for us." We hid in the ditch until the car went by. An elderly man with a handlebar mustache drove it, an old Jaguar with rust spots on the side. "I'm thirsty," said Titus, but we had already passed the spring in the ditch. I searched for that look in his eyes, but he was fine. "We're almost home, buddy," Ted said. I glanced at him. He muttered, "Mrs. Neukom won't tell."

But when we got home Mom grabbed Ted and me by the earlobes and marched us into her bedroom and paddled us bent double across the quilted bed. We bit our lower lips so we would not cry, but Ted was better; I held out almost until the end, until she said, "Why on earth did you do that? You used to like Mrs. Neukom. She always let you play with her monkey. I honestly would like to know what got into you."

We said nothing. I was shivering and trying at least to be silent so Ted would not notice.

Then Ted said, "We thought she killed Judas."

Mom demanded, "What are you talking about?"

Ted bit his thumbnail.

Mom said, "I don't know what's gotten into you boys."

When we came out Titus said, "I heard you guys get it." I ignored him and went to my room. He followed me in and said, "I'm sorry if you're mad at me, but it's Mrs. Neukom's fault."

Mom made us clean out Mrs. Neukom's pool. Mrs. Neukom got out all the old rusty poles and explained in a quiet gravelly voice how they worked, and we fit them together and dipped out all the moss and flung it over the back fence and scrubbed down the sides. Mrs. Neukom was inside, and sometimes we could see her through the kitchen window pouring a drink from a clear bottle and stirring it with her finger. She came out and showed us how to hook up the vacuum, and we vacuumed out the pool. The machine clogged twice and we had to turn it off and clean the stinking brackish sludge from the tubes and flush them out with the hose.

"We shouldn't have to do all this," Ted whispered. "It's not fair. We already got out more than we put in." He wiped his brow, and I agreed, "Mom hates us. She wants us to be Mrs. Neukom's slaves." Titus came over and played in the yard and watched us for a while, but he got bored and went home. The pool was clean now, but the water was cloudy and yellowish; Mrs. Neukom had bought some jugs of chlorine and showed us how to dump the right amount in the water. When she talked she expelled her boozy breath in our faces. We poured the chlorine in the pool, and she made us wash our hands with soap at the outside tap before we touched our eyes. Then she gave us each a glass of ice and some Cragmont orange drink that had gone flat. "You boys finish that up and skedaddle," she said. We glugged down the orange drink and went home, wiping our mouths on the backs of our hands.

The next night after dinner Mom said, "I'm proud of you boys. Mrs. Neukom said you did a fine job cleaning out her pool. Not a word of complaint. And she sent over a treat."

Mom handed us each a chocolate bar with almonds.

"Why does Titus get one?" I asked. "He didn't help."

"Because he didn't throw dirt clods in the first place," Mom said.

Ted told Titus and me as we watched "Gunsmoke," "I'm not going to eat mine. She's an old slavedriver. I'm going to flush mine down the toilet."

Titus unwrapped his candy bar and ate a bite.

Ted said, "Come on. Let's all go in at commercial and flush them down the toilet."

"Nuh-uh," Titus said. He grinned, and there was chocolate on his teeth.

Ted could not change our minds, so he decided to eat his

candy bar. "You two are so greedy," he said with his mouth full.

That night when we went to bed there was still a glow in the western sky, and I could not sleep. The insects gathered on my screen. Titus dropped off at once, and I listened to him snore. Mom and Dad were talking in the living room and drinking iced tea, and I heard their low laughter through the wall. I got up and dressed. My candy bar was hidden in a cigar box under my bed, and I lay on my belly and retrieved it and stuck it in my pocket. I sneaked out the back door.

The moon shone on the horizon, and the Joshua trees cast long, twisted shadows on the sand. Down on the highway a deputy's car raced along with its siren blaring, and that started up the coyotes. They howled and yipped up in the hills. I wondered how the brothers at the priory could sleep with coyotes creeping around in their pear orchard. I was scared, but I thought, Coyotes are just dogs, and they eat crickets and toads and rabbits and garbage out behind restaurants but not people; they are afraid of us. I went to the creosote bush near the house and left the candy bar as bait, to lure the coyote back to his den.

Famous People

Lowell Ely, who was often mistaken for someone famous himself and even signed an autograph once on Miami Beach, knew lots of famous people. How many, he refused to say. Maybe all of them—at least that was what one of his housemates, Angus Beachy, suggested before the tragedy (which was reported on the front page of the *Miami Herald* and even warranted articles in papers as diverse as *Sovet Uzebekistoni* and *Mysore Prabha*). But then Angus was easily impressed, and besides, Lowell had already admitted he had never met Barbra Streisand. "She's not that famous anyway," Angus insisted. "You can't really count her. I had never even heard of her before *Yentl* came out." Erica Crane snapped, "You had never heard of anybody before Lowell told you about them," and Angus, a conservative Mennonite, took this as a grudging compliment.

At any rate, even Erica had to admit that Lowell's list of acquaintances was impressive—"Assuming he's telling the truth," she said. Robert Goulet. Bob Hope. Sting. Dolly Parton's sister. Phyllis George. Garrison Keillor. Meryl Streep. David Hartman. Michael Jackson (who had owned a pet llama, Lowell said, until his two Irish wolfhounds hunted it down in a back corner of his Encino estate, killed it, and left its partially devoured carcass under an oleander). Lowell even knew the guy you seemed to see everywhere on television nowadays, the one who, dressed as a doughboy in a Ford or Chevrolet commercial several years ago, sang while marching in place:

> Over there! Over there!
> Tell the cars over there to beware!

Like the rest of his housemates, Lowell attended the University of Miami. They lived in a bad part of town, in a neighborhood where you occasionally ran a red light rather than sit with your car idling in front of the bars and shops where the unemployed kids hung out, lest they become too excited and begin throwing bottles and rocks. (After this happened to Lowell one day, he mused, "I wonder if they thought I was somebody else?") But unlike the others, Lowell seldom watched television. He spent most of his time away from school in the backyard, reclining in a lawn chair and reading (this semester, at any rate) *The Norton Anthology of Anonymous Lyrics* while he pulled up tufts of the wide-bladed Florida grass with his toes; after dark, he holed up in his room, revising his annotated bibliography of forty major postmodernist poets. Lowell was an English major. Whenever he left his bedroom and walked blinking into the living room, he would pause a moment, especially if it was a muggy evening and the windows were open to the singing of the cicadas, and stare at the black-and-white television screen. Then he would leave the room.

Terri Mackay once said, "You can turn it on if you like."

"Oh, no, thanks," said Lowell.

But if the television was on, he might pause for a few minutes longer and watch the show with the others, the corners of his mouth twitching slightly as he suppressed a smile.

"I know him," he would say as blandly as possible.

"Sure," said Erica. "Paul Newman, huh?"

"No, of course not. George Kennedy."

"See," Erica said to Angus. "There's somebody else he admits he doesn't know."

Angus ignored her. "Who's George Kennedy?" he asked.

Terri said, "Him."

"The old guy beating up Paul Newman," Lowell said.

"No kidding?"

"Stay down, Luke," George Kennedy said.

"I'm serious. He and my dad used to play backgammon all the time."

There was no denying that Lowell looked famous, although as Erica once said, scathingly, within earshot of Lowell, "Of course, we're all from the Midwest. How would we know if celebrities really look like Lowell?" Lowell flashed his dazzling smile. He was from Los Angeles. He moved in after Kirk, whose father was crushed in the jaws of a mechanical white whale in an amusement park on the New Jersey shore, had to drop out and tend the family business. When Lowell showed up at the house—a tall, blond student checking the address against a card he had removed from the bulletin board at the campus housing office—the others were surprised to see that he brought with him a duffel bag of red, green, and black canvas, marked on the sides with a Rastafarian Lion of Judah, and a surfboard in a black case, which he carried in and set on the couch. "Is that my bedroom in there?" he asked. The others glanced at one another and decided to dispense with the interview and the twelve pages of notes they had taken on other potential housemates. Lowell stayed. Whenever he strolled along Biscayne Boulevard wearing sunglasses and his faded jeans and Hawaiian shirt, elegant Latinas in spike heels and dresses that were tight at the knees, and businessmen carrying rhinoceros skin briefcases, faltered in their conversations as they passed and stared, trying to place him.

One day Lowell decided to catch a bus to Little Havana and wander around, and Angus asked if he could tag along. Angus was short and muscular, without a trace of whiskers on his childlike face. He was from a black-bumper Mennonite household: his family painted over the chrome on their cars, considering it worldly. The two cut through a small park, passing the rows of tables where Cuban men sat playing dominoes. Some of the men wore Panama hats, and the backs of their shirts were sweat-speckled, revealing the singlets underneath. Lowell and Angus visited a tiny lunch counter and ordered Cuban coffee, which cost only a dime apiece. The waitress spoke no English. Lowell said, "Café cubano, please," and pointed to a man drinking a demitasse at the end of the counter. Angus said, "Me too." She looked at him. Angus pointed to the man, and she nodded. She looked over her shoulder at Lowell as she made the coffee and averted her eyes when he stared back. She brought the coffee, as bitter as espresso, along with the small glasses of ice water that always accompanied it, and set them on the counter.

A well-dressed brunette sat down on a stool two seats over from Lowell, ordered in Spanish, and then stared at him. Angus nudged Lowell, who smiled. Angus inhaled the humid aroma of his coffee, ventured to sip the dark brew, and decided he disliked it.

"Excuse me," the woman said to Lowell. "Have I seen you somewhere before?" Lowell shrugged, and the woman immediately said, "I know that's probably a silly question."

"Not at all."

"You remind me of somebody—I can't recall who, though."

"I have a familiar face."

The woman handed Lowell a card. He glanced at it and set it on the counter, where a corner of the paper began soaking up spilled coffee. The card read, "Becky Gabriel / Talent Associates," and included an address and phone number.

Becky Gabriel said, "Would you be interested in taking a screen test?"

"No, thank you."

A man in a polyester suit and a bolo tie sitting beside Angus said, "Don't tell me you drink that Cuban coffee without ice water. That will burn holes in your gut."

Angus said, "Oh, really?"

"Don't be scared off by the sound of it," Becky Gabriel said. "It's nothing, really. I'm trying to cast some parts in a television show that's filmed locally. It could earn you some money."

"Huh."

"Have you ever done any acting?"

"No."

The man pointed a thick finger at Angus' coffee cup. "I'm from Puerto Rico, and I can't stand that stuff. Cubans are crazy. That gives you heart attacks if you drink too much. I can't say that too loud in here, though."

"Wouldn't you be willing to at least give it a try?" Becky Gabriel was saying. She had slid one seat closer to Lowell. The man tugged on Angus' sleeve. "Who's your friend?" he whispered. "I won't tell anyone."

"He's nobody."

"I see the agent wants him." He was looking at the card.

"I guess so."

"What's his name?" the man said.

"Don Johnson," said Angus. It was the first name that occurred to him. He blushed.

"Ah. That name is familiar."

Becky Gabriel asked Angus, "Did you say something?"

"I was talking to him."

"Let's go, Angus," Lowell said. He stood up, tucking his shirt in at the back.

"Wait," Becky Gabriel said.

Lowell walked out the door. Angus paid for the coffee and ran out after him. When he emerged on the bright, hot sidewalk, Lowell was already jogging across the street and dodging traffic, thumping once on the roof of a yellow Dodge Dart that honked at him. Angus caught up with him on the opposite curb. They boarded the next bus they came to, even though it was not heading in their direction. Angus told Lowell about the Puerto Rican man, but Lowell was pensive and silent and gave only a slight, hurt smile as he stared out the window at the royal palms along the road and, across Biscayne Bay, at the old deco hotels of Miami Beach, magnified in the humid, bluish, lambent atmosphere that hung over the water and the mangrove islets. Then Angus realized where Lowell was looking: at his own reflection in the glass.

"I hate it when that happens," he said.

The bus ground to a stop amid a miasma of blue exhaust beside a salmon-colored stucco house, its weedy yard surrounded by a chain-link fence. Two boys appeared and started hollering—they scrambled up the fence, which was seven feet high and topped with barbed wire, and began shooting at the bus with Transformer robots they had turned into guns. Lowell smiled at the boys, but his complexion was ashen. The bus deposited an elderly woman on the curb to waddle off with her grocery bag, then rolled on, and palm leaves swept the windows. It was Ash Wednesday, but Lowell and Angus did not know this, and when Officer Joel Gallegos arrived at the house with a cross still faintly traced on his forehead, Angus imagined the man had somehow bruised himself breaking up a fistfight in a bar.

That night a celebrity gala event, involving a number of famous people, appeared on television, broadcast from Washington, D.C. The others were eating popcorn and watching the show when the door to Lowell's room opened, and Erica said, "Don't ask him about anybody. He's only waiting to show off." Lowell walked blinking through the room into the kitchen and opened the refrigerator, which cast a pale glow on the warped linoleum floor, vanishing as he shut the door. He returned to the living room, carrying a can of cherry cola, and sat on an arm of the couch. Martin Sheen was on television, doing a one-man impersonation of God creating the universe, to Angus' vague discomfiture. "I'm lonely," said Martin Sheen. Lowell wiped his mouth and softly whistled a few bars from "Ride of the Valkyries." "Shhh," said Erica. Lowell laughed and said, "Sorry."

He plucked a thread from the couch and dangled it in Erica's ear.

"Lowell, please."

"It's just that you're so irresistible. Look at that lovely freckled neck."

He leaned over and tried to kiss her nape. His breath tickled the hairs along the edge of her scalp.

"I'm driving you wild, I can tell."

"You smell like bourbon." Erica moved down the couch.

Lowell said, "Hi, Angus."

Angus blurted out, "Do you know that guy?"

"Angus!" Erica said.

Lowell sat up. "Who? Oh, yes, I know Marty, as a matter of fact."

Erica removed a hairpin from the bun atop her head and shook her hair free. "All right," she said in a tremulous voice. "Let's just watch this."

Ronald Reagan appeared onstage. He told a joke, and the audience roared and applauded. The joke was about Congress, but nobody remembered it afterward. The camera caught Tip O'Neill laughing and blowing his nose in his handkerchief. Then it showed Reagan.

"Oh, shut up," Erica said.

"I didn't say a word," Lowell said.

"I'm talking to Ronnie."

"Only his wife calls him that, Erica."

Angus leaned forward to where he could see around Erica. Lowell winked at him.

"Do you know President Reagan?" Angus asked.

"Angus! We agreed—"

"Nobody agreed, Erica. You just announced it. Lowell, do you know him?"

"We're just nodding acquaintances."

"How did you meet?"

"Cecil B. De Mille's daughter introduced us at the Beverly Hills Hotel one day."

"Gosh."

"Yep."

Sirens were keening out on the streets. Lowell walked to the window and snapped the insects clinging to the screen, launching them into the darkness, flitting motes of light swallowed up in the void. He leaned forward and said with his lips against the screen, "Sounds wild out there." Officer Gallegos was fastening his seat belt and starting the engine of his patrol car.

"What a talented bunch," President Reagan said.

"I know," said Erica. "I hope it's not another Overtown."

Lowell said, "Maybe they'll burn down the school."

Erica glanced at him. "I left my sunglasses in one of my classes."

Lowell walked to the front door. He called, "I'm going to get some fresh air."

Michael Jackson was on television. No one answered.

Lowell stepped outside. In retrospect, the others said in their statements, they seemed to remember him calling out, "What are you doing here?" or perhaps, "How long have you been in town?" before he even had a chance to close the door. The three gunshots they were sure of, however, and a police weapons expert testified that he found three shells on the front porch and three bullets in that vicinity: one embedded in the doorpost, one in the flower bed beside the front window, and a third under Lowell's jawbone. The murderer would fire his Colt .45 semiautomatic pistol twice more, inside. The reports were loud but sounded remarkably false, like firecrackers blown off in tin cans.

Angus said, "What on earth was that?"

The door swung open, and a pale man entered. His Hawaiian shirt was unbuttoned, and underneath he wore a green T-shirt. He wore baggy white hospital pants and a pair of slippers, and held a pistol.

The girls gasped.

"Stay seated," the man said. His face was terribly familiar.

"Who are you?" Angus asked. "What happened to Lowell?"

"I just bumped him off," the man said. He pretended to blow smoke off the barrel of his pistol and said, "Bang."

Terri started to cry. "We're pacifists," she said.

"What are you watching?" the man said. His face was familiar.

Angus stood up and stammered, "I'm going to help Lowell." His ears were scarlet, and he glanced at the man with the gun. The man said, "Sit down," and pointed the gun at Angus. Angus froze. He licked his lips. Then he said, "Didn't you try to kill somebody famous before?"

"Yes," the man said, crossing his arms but keeping the pistol pointed at Angus.

"Was it Jodie Foster?"

"Angus!" Erica said.

"No," the gunman said simultaneously, in exasperation. "Now sit down."

Angus was trembling. His teeth chattered. "I'm going to check on Lowell," he said and walked out past the gunman. The man turned and aimed at the back of Angus' head and sighted down the barrel. The girls screamed. Angus froze. After a second he forced himself to walk on to the front door. The gunman sniffed and let his arm fall to his side. Angus left.

"Aw, what the hell," the man said. "I'm going to surrender myself to the police anyway." He looked flustered, and he turned to Erica. "Do you remember me?"

"Yes. But your name slips my mind."

"Not even my first name?"

"Um, Frank?"

The man shot the television screen, exploding a Grape-Nuts commercial into a shower of glass. Angus stuck his head back through the door. Tears were running down his cheeks. "What happened?" he said. "Is everybody all right?"

Terri was sobbing hysterically. Erica's face was scarlet. She hugged Terri and said in a small voice, "Okay."

"Okay," the gunman sneered. He shot another round at the hollow, smoking television, then glowered at Erica. "The least you could do is try to remind me."

"Remember you," said Erica.

"Remember," the man said. "Yes."

On Freedom

Harv Ruschke saw the police car cruising down the alley only an instant before the officer spotted him through the gap where a board was missing in the gate, which Grandfather Larson had broken by letting an ax slip through his grip while chopping wood ("Who the hell has been using this with grease all over his hands?" he shouted in his Norwegian accent, but Harv did not answer because he was inside carrying his grandmother to the bathtub), and although Harv had a second to fling his noon chucks into the ivy before the policeman looked, he thought, That cop might glance over any second and see the black-polished wood flying and the glint of the sun on the chain; besides, this is private property, and he can't enter the yard without my permission. So Harv continued to whirl the two rods linked by chain, swiftly, around his neck and torso, between his legs, the noon chucks whirring with a sound like the fluttering of a mallard flushed from a brake: a sound reminiscent of boyhood and eastern Washington and the scent of snow in the air, which always set the geese and ducks migrating further south (but never here; the birds must circumnavigate the entire Los Angeles Basin) under the black, laden sky of a late autumn afternoon—unlike the still, sunny winter sky overhead. And it almost worked. The officer did not even glance at the gap, and the patrol car flashed black-white-black past the gate. Then it stopped. Brake lights glowed, the car reversed, and the policeman gaped, his arm hanging out the window, shook his head incredulously, and spoke into his radio. Harv ceased his exercises and, his hands on his hips, let the noon chucks dangle at his side. He was breathing hard.

The policeman called, "You know, them things are illegal in California."

"No kidding?" said Harv. "I'm new here. I'm from Washington."

"I'd be willing to bet they're illegal in DC too."

"Yakima," said Harv. "I'm from Washington State."

The policeman turned off the engine and got out of the car,

leaving his radio dangling from the window. "Why don't you drop them and come on out here where we can have a little talk?"

Harv jingled the chain in his fingertips, and a sudden urge which he suppressed set his heart beating faster, and his skin, already glossy with sweat, broke out in gooseflesh.

The policeman hunched over and peered through the gap. "Come on out here," he said, picking at a splinter, "and drop your weapon."

"Weapon," said Harv. He stood with his legs spread, shirtless, the waistband of his jeans damp as he tightened his abdominal muscles.

"What's that?"

"This is private property. You can't order me off."

The officer reached for his radio and requested a backup unit. He was a thin-shouldered man with gross lips and nose, like a clay self-portrait displayed in a high school art class. Releasing the radio to clatter against the side of the car, he stepped forward and rested a foot on a crossbar in the gate.

"Get the hell over here. Now."

The oleander along the inside of the fence sibilated in a gentle breath of wind: resisssssst. The bush dithered and flickered in the soft winter light.

Harv said, "You can't order me out of my own yard." He flipped the noon chucks in the air and grabbed one of the rods.

The policeman unhooked the clasp on his black leather holster with a flick of his middle finger. He drew a revolver past his gut and stuck it through the space between the boards. "Drop the damn noon chucks if you don't want to be shot in your own backyard. That's right. Now come on over here. Attaboy. Now unlatch the gate and come on through. You make one move for your pockets and I'll blow a hole in your skull."

As the officer made him lie facedown in a compost heap of smoking wet grass clippings in the back alley, Harv heard a siren come around the corner and saw a squad car flashing its blue-and-red disks—"Put your head down!" Harv heard, thinking, Shoving my face in the ripe rotting grass: "Shit, man, you're a walking arsenal." A door slammed.

"This punk"—grunting, he twists this punk's arms behind him and handcuffs him—"was in the yard here whipping around this set of noon chucks, jiggling them like he was going to use them and everything. Refused to drop them. Look what I'm finding here: a kung fu arsenal in his pockets. Chinese throwing stars—whatever you call these." A rap on the wooden gate. "Jeez, that's sharp. Look at the way it cuts into wood. Real tough guy, aren't you, kid?"

Then followed a comment that Harv missed because of a fly that buzzed up almost into his ear canal, then flitted away, and a reading of his rights in a voice rendered bored, ponderous, toneless, by innumerable repetitions of the same words printed in large type on a dog-eared card, which the cop must have retrieved from his breast pocket; the reading lacked the drama of an actor's well-crafted just wrath and television's staging:

OFFICER HILL
(Kneeing suspect in the groin)
You have the right to remain silent. Got that, sucker? And, jack, anything you say can be used against you in a court of law.

The policeman pulled Harv up and stood him on his feet, the backup officer, a woman, even brushing the grass from his face with light strokes of her fingertips, and Harv realized that they intended to go through with it: it will take me a couple of days to get out on bail, and Grandpa (assuming he returns tonight) will have to hire a nurse burly enough to hoist fat old Grandma out of bed and get her to the wheelchair. And of course I will stand up Kristi tomorrow night. He smiled at the policewoman, a brunette with a winning, childish gap between two teeth, but she looked away.

By the time they arrived downtown, a voice on the radio had informed the officer of Harv's record up in Washington, including the fourteen months of back payments he owed in attorney's fees and fines and restitution for throwing a tool-box through a junk dealer's plate glass window. It was a stupid conviction, and Harv was amazed they knew about it down here. He had sold his 1966 Valiant for $350 and invested the money to help start the store, but the owner, Steve, ended up firing him and refused to pay back the money. Harv's father, a soft-spoken school bus driver and an elder in the Missionary Baptist Church, swore for what was probably the first time in his life when Steve left the stand: "Bastard," he said in a loud voice. The judge, fellow member of the Lions Club, peered over his glasses and said, "Order. Hold your tongue, Amos." Harv's mother was too stunned even to nudge his dad.

The car was descending the ramp to the underground garage. The steel grill was closing behind them. They rounded a curve, and a concrete wall cut off the daylight. Brake lights on another car glowed through the windshield, and Harv thought, It is always a surrender, leaving something behind—then the notion he was grasping for vanished. You gave in to the tedium, the uniforms, the guards and smart-ass trusties and snitch jackets. You never saw clocks and sensed only a rising hunger, clipped momentarily by a meal. The prisoners paced when they were restless. You rose and ate breakfast and paced and then napped and ate lunch and slept some more. They would come with dinner, and you knew that the day was on the downhill slope, and you ate meatloaf and gravy and boiled olive-colored peas and potatoes. Maybe they gave you a cookie and lukewarm coffee. The food in some places was not too bad if you had been unemployed and cut off from food stamps. It depended on what you were used to. You paced in the cell after dinner, read in the feeble illumination of the common area, smoked one cigarette, played a few hands of poker. Maybe you won some candy money and a couple more cigarettes or only lost a few quarters. You went to bed before lockdown and slept ten hours. Harv jerked his wrists against his cuffs (the cop turned and said, "Watch it back there, ace") and thought as always how flimsy they seemed, like some toy you buy at a carnival and pick open with a key from a sardine tin. Still, watch the others. You are not bad-looking (Kristi at least says so), and you are shirtless and sweaty and itching with flecks of grass. Harv was agitated. He was ready to fight.

The officer parked and opened the car door. "Come on," he said. "Let's go."

The booking area was large and dirty and filled with naked prisoners standing in line waiting to be checked in. The men stood in front of a caged area where a fat sergeant sat humming to himself as he scribbled on a prisoner's report, then took the man's hand, shyly, like a groom placing a ring on the finger of his beloved, and one by one dipped the prisoner's fingers on an inky pad and fingerprinted him. Harv's officer said, "Got another one for you, Bill." A guard grunted and accepted some papers the officer handed him. The officer left. Bill—a burly but weak-chinned man whose blondish gray hair was slicked across his balding head—slipped his billy club back in his belt, fished a key chain from his pocket, and unlocked Harv's handcuffs.

"Strip," he said.

Harv lifted his legs, standing on one and then the other like a crane, and pulled his tennis shoes from his feet by the heels. He removed his socks (the tops were mismatched: one red-striped, the other blue-and-gold) and stuffed them in his shoes. The floor was sticky. Harv wriggled his toes and grimaced. The guard Bill was standing behind him. Harv turned to look at him—the man was reading the police report. "What the hell are Chinese stars?" he muttered. Harv brushed the lint from his toenails. "Get your pants off," Bill said.

"Oooo," said a prisoner. "The man gets to look up another asshole."

The prisoners laughed. An old drunk with shoulder-length hair and a tangled beard shook his head and said, "Woooeee!"

"Who said that?" Bill asked. He drew his billy club and walked up the line. The men quieted. "Who the hell said that?"

The guard slapped his club against his palm. The old man was nodding and mumbling to himself. Bill said, "Pretty funny, isn't it, old man?" The drunk opened his eyes wide and looked at the guard. Bill jammed the club into his ribs and knocked the wind out of him—the man bent double and wheezed. Harv stuffed his underwear in his pants pocket and rolled his shoes up in his jeans. A short, muscular guard whose head was shaved accepted the wad of clothing and carried it to a slot in the cage.

Bill locked the cuffs back on Harv. "Get in line."

The man in front of Harv must have been six-foot-ten, covered with tattoos, including a hunting dog on one buttock that was chasing a fox around the lobe of the man's cheek and into his cleft. And his back was covered with a tattoo of a nude woman bathing in a stream, surrounded by stars and spiders and skulls and crossbones. The man craned his neck to survey Harv. He wore a scruffy beard, thin on the left, and his right eye was puffy with a sty. He said, "Hey, kid. What's your name?"

"Ruschke."

"Ruschke? No kidding. People ever call you Rush?"

"No."

"That's what my friends call me, man. Rush."

"Oh, really."

"Shit, yes."

"No talking in line," said the short guard, prodding Rush with his billy club.

"All right. Fucking back off. Shit."

Bill said, "Just knock him upside the head if he sasses you, Neal."

"Hey, fuck you," Rush muttered, but the guards, distracted by the arrival of another prisoner, did not hear.

Rush's hands opened and clenched into fists. Then he relaxed and watched the new man undress. Other prisoners watched too. Were they watching me as I pulled my shorts down over my hips? thought Harv. No, of course: who said that—slapping his palm with the club and preparing to open a gash in the head of someone who confessed. The new prisoner's hair was parted in the middle and carefully combed, and he hunched over and clasped his hands in front of himself, as if to hide his groin, until Bill handcuffed him once again. Rush grinned when the man glanced at him, then looked away.

Harv looked around at the three windowed walls of the room. You could see what were probably intended as holding cells, filled now with men dressed in coveralls who shuffled about, played cards, watched the incoming prisoners through the Plexiglas windows, or lay on mattresses on the floor.

Bill burst out laughing. "Raping your wife?" he said, waving the new prisoner's papers. "How do you rape your own wife? Did you attack her out in an alley behind a dumpster?"

The men in line laughed. Bill grinned at them as he escorted the rapist to the back of the line.

"What?" said Bill.

"No," answered the man. He was flabby and white, his gut creased horizontally as if he spent most of his time sitting, and wisps of hair encircled his nipples.

"Where, then?"

"In our bedroom."

"Judas fucking priest," said Rush to the ceiling.

"I guess we're all in trouble," said Neal. "I do that about four times a week."

"At least," Bill guffawed.

An hour later the corpulent guard behind the cage booked and fingerprinted Harv. He glanced at some papers on the counter beside him and kept humming the same tune; occasionally he supplied lyrics in falsetto: "Suicide, suicide," he sang. Harv said, "What?" and the deputy became flustered and said, "Talk only when you're spoken to." He passed a pair of plastic slippers through a slot in the cage, and Harv dropped them on the floor and stepped into them. "No socks?" he joked. The guard said, "Shut your face, smart-ass." He spat chewing tobacco juice into a paper cup. "What size coveralls you wear? We're all out of thirty-two waist. You want bigger or smaller? Check. Here you go." Then Harv asked if he could make his own phone call, and though the guard at first refused, when Harv explained that he was supposed to be taking care of his sick grandmother, the guard stopped looking over his shoulder and met his gaze and sighed. "Another sob story," he said. Harv grinned. The deputy said, "So how come your granddad isn't home?" Harv said, "He was out of town." The fat man sighed and said, "Aw, what the hell. But someone will have to make the call for you and listen in on the conversation."

"No problem," Harv said.

Harv sat on a cold metal chair while a guard dialed; he rang Kristi's number first but no one answered. The guard drummed his fingers on the desk as he listened to the ringing. After the fifth ring he hung up.

"I guess your grandma's going to have to take care of herself."

"Wait," said Harv. "Try one more number. Maybe my grandpa's home by now."

"All right." On the third ring Grandfather Larson answered the phone.

"Hello?"

"Hello, Mr. Ruschke?"

"No. The name is Larson."

"Do you have a grandson named Harv Ruschke?"

"Yes."

The guard explained that Harv had been arrested.

"Damn that bloody boy," said Mr. Larson.

"Your grandson's on the line, Mr. Larson, and he'd like to ask you something."

"Harv's there?"

"Yes, sir."

"Then put him on."

"Go ahead, Ruschke."

"Hello, Grandpa."

"Damn you, boy. What the hell is going on?"

"I'll tell you about it later, Grandpa. Listen, it will probably take me a couple of days to get out on bail, and I wanted to make sure that Grandma—"

"Which you'll probably expect me to pay."

"What?"

"You think I'll bail you out again, eh? I've a good mind to leave you in there and teach you a lesson. Grandpa gets back from a trip to Reno, and maybe he is looking for a way to throw away the money he won, bailing a mule-headed boy out of jail, is that what you figure? Who's supposed to take care of your grandmother while you're locked up? Mmm? Do you ever stop and think about these things before you go and get yourself arrested?"

"Why the hell do you think I called? I wanted to make sure she's got somebody there."

"Oh, that's very thoughtful of you."

"Mr. Larson, I'm afraid we're going to have to cut this conversation off."

"Grandpa, before you go, why don't you try Kristi? If she can't come in and help tomorrow, she might know of someone who can."

"Kristi, eh? You know, you have her worried half to death. She's been calling all over trying to track you down. It's humiliating. I should think one of these times you yourself would be a bit embarrassed by it all."

"Hang up, Ruschke," said the deputy. He rubbed his eyes.

"Grandpa, I got to go. Tell Grandma I love her."

"Good-bye," the old man said. The line went dead.

Harv and the guard hung up. Harv looked at the table and shrugged. "He's like that sometimes," he said. The guard pushed his chair back from the table. "Let's get you to your cell."

He led Harv down the hall through a barred steel door that was flaking white paint. The walls were pale turquoise. The color was supposed to soothe you. Even here the prisoners had somehow managed to scratch graffiti on the walls. They came to a door that opened onto a long, narrow common room in between two rows of eight-by-ten-foot cells: five on one side and four on the other, along with a shower. A color television was on in the corner: a man in a cowboy hat wrestled a Bengal tiger in a lot full of used cars with prices on their windshields. The man's hat fell off. "Here's your blanket," said the guard. "You're in number four. Lockdown's at ten o'clock."

"When's dinner?" said Harv.

"You missed it. These guys finished licking their trays clean an hour ago."

"Hey, wait a minute. I was standing out in line there."

"Tough shit. We don't serve nobody till he checks in. Breakfast's at eight. You can wait till then without starving." He slammed the door.

A group of men was playing cards around a table bolted to the concrete floor in the center of the room. They looked at Harv, and he spat and said, "Son of a bitch." He held the gaze of a gangly prisoner, bald on the left side of his head, whose neck, left ear, and face (the left side was worse) were covered in pinkish blotches, with scar tissue forming a tight orifice around one eye. The man laid a jack of diamonds on the table. "What you staring at, white boy?" he demanded. Harv said, "I ain't figured it out yet." The scarred man said, "Hey, fuck you," but he looked away at the seal-tank green wall. Harv entered cell number four and tossed his blanket on a mattress that lay on the floor; both of the bunks, already claimed, were piled with paperback books and magazines and rumpled blankets. "And keep your fucking paws off my stuff or I'll kick your ass!"

the man shouted. Someone told him, "Pay attention, Jimmy."
Harv thought, Damn. Stuck in a cell with a ghoul, although I
could take him, skinny bastard, and he knows it. A pile of pink
mattress stuffing lay in the corner like a sleeping hounddog.
Cigarette butts, coverless magazines, and paperback books
were scattered across the floor of the cell. Against the vomit-
flecked back wall stood a toilet unit with a sink built into the
top, of gray plastic, rust-streaked at the bolts, spigots, and
flush fixture.

The other residents had decorated the walls with cata-
log photographs of pubescent girls in their underwear: one
pressed a doll to her breasts; all of them were in clean bed-
rooms with spreads and pillows on the beds; dressed in slips
or panties and bras; at slumber parties, talking wistfully about
boys; or alone, staring beyond the camera, their glossy lips
parted. Other magazine ads depicted women in various stages
of undress (one completely naked but tastefully photographed
from behind), and in one picture a half- (but stylishly) dressed
couple made love, evidently amid the scent of the perfume or
aphrodisiac named at the bottom of the page. The air stank of
vomited cheap wine. Laughter came from the table outside,
"Damn you fucking cheats! Give me that!" followed by the
sound of a scuffle and the hissed words, "God's coming." Himself? A visitation: he came into the room and stood among
them. Grandma would believe it. "God": their accent catches
you off guard sometimes. Harv reentered the common room.
Someone was shuffling a deck of cards for the men at the
table, and no one spoke. A group of chicanos in number eight
chattered like charismatics.

As the guard peered through the observation window from
the hall, Harv sat down at the far end of the table from Jimmy
and begged a cigarette from another prisoner, the rapist. He
lit up and filled his lungs with smoke—savoring the tobacco
taste, the gradual numbing of the tip of his tongue.

The rapist slid closer and said, "What's your name?"

"Harv."

"Harv? I'm Willis."

"Hiya, Willis. How you doing?"

"Fine, thank you." Willis rested his arms on the table. His forearm brushed Harv's hip, and he said, "Excuse me." Harv was sitting on the table with his feet on the bench, and when he tapped his cigarette on his knee, ash speckled Willis' hair.

"What did they get you for?" said Willis, stifling a belch. Jimmy glanced up from his card game.

"Assault one," said Harv.

"No kidding?" Willis made a gesture that knocked his cigarette from his mouth. The butt fell to the table, and he picked it up and then brushed the flecks of ash from the table, where someone had scratched a row of swastikas and the words, "United White Peoples Party." The ash drifted to his lap. "Who did you beat up? Or did you? Maybe you're innocent."

"My grandpa."

"How about that." He rubbed his nose and said, "Why?"

"Why did you rape your wife, man? It's none of your business."

"I'm sorry. I didn't mean to pry."

Harv shrugged, emitting a jet of smoke from his nostrils.

"I didn't really rape my wife, you know. I may have gotten a bit rough, but, I mean, this is ludicrous," he laughed, shaking his head and expelling choppy breaths with each syllable, "raping your own wife."

Jimmy said, "Hey, nobody gives a flying rat's ass whether you done it, so why don't you just shut your mouth?"

Willis leaned over and scraped the ember from his cigarette butt on the floor. He got up and walked around the room, looking in the corners, perhaps for a trash can. After one lap he touched the tip of the butt twice—briefly, then keeping his finger there for a moment—and dropped it in his pocket. He stood in the doorway of the cell across from Harv's, number three, where a prisoner slept on the lower bunk, enshrouded in a blanket, his arm hanging to the floor.

"My cell mate likes to sleep," said Willis.

"Hunh," said Harv, thumbing through a Western that some-one had left on the table.

"Do you know who he is?" said Willis. "Big guy with the tattoos?"

"Rush."

"Yes, that's his name. Did you see that one tattoo on his back, of a whaler harpooning a sperm whale? Incredible detail."

"Sperm?" said a small redheaded prisoner with a vandyke (the first word he had spoken all evening). "Did somebody say sperm?"

A man who crouched on the bench opposite Jimmy said, "You need somebody to explain what that is, Pete?"

"Fuck you, man."

Willis laughed and looked around at the others. They went on with their card game. He said, "No, seriously, the thing I thought of was, see, I'm a teacher, and I took a class on a field trip to Catalina this one time—"

Jimmy slapped down his card and said, "I thought I told you to shut your mouth. Some of us is trying to concentrate."

Willis' smiling gaze dropped to his slippers, and he re-turned to his cell, fished the cigarette butt from his pocket, and tossed it in the toilet bowl. He struggled to scale the top bunk without stepping on Rush's bed, but Rush awoke and rolled over and pulled the blanket back. He watched Willis with a grin and yawned, spraying a fine mist in the light of the cell.

"Lookee here," Rush said. "Company."

Harv set down the Western and entered his cell about half an hour before lockdown, though he decided on the prob-able time in retrospect. In jail he figured time by reflection and deduction until he had been incarcerated long enough to recover his innate time sense. He would note that the guard was slamming the cell doors, one by one, of those not prescient enough to shut their own doors a moment before he entered the common room; it was now ten o'clock, and it must have been (bearing in mind the languorous movement of time in jail) thirty minutes ago that Jimmy and Rush were chatting on the bunk there. The two sat side by side on Jimmy's bunk. Jimmy patted Rush's thigh with his hand turned upside down, the middle finger extended toward Harv. "What about pretty boy here?"

"Nah," said Rush. "Leave him alone. Rush here is my friend."

"What you talking about?" said Jimmy.

"His name's Rush too. Didn't you know that? And me and him are buddies, ain't we, Rush?"

"Damn right," said Harv. He sat on his mattress and crossed his legs like a Buddha figure, removing his slippers. Yet he was alert. Check your path of escape. Anyone in the doorway? No. Be ready to spring. You can't fight the two of them in an enclosed space. No room for movement. Harv massaged his feet, seemingly uninterested, but watching their shadows on the ground and the edge of his mattress.

"His name ain't Rush," Jimmy objected, as if the question rode on this alone.

Harv looked up and held Jimmy's gaze. The eye puckered.

Jimmy shifted, pulled a strip of blanket out from under him, and wrapped it around his hand. He muttered, "They sure as hell ain't two Rushes in one jail. I never met another Rush before in my life."

Rush shoved him with his elbow. "Hey, fucking shut up, all right?" He got up. "You coming over?"

"Yeah," said Jimmy. "Just give me a second." He rolled up an extra blanket and lay it on his mattress, along with a pile of books and magazines, and covered the pile with his blanket.

"Don't touch this," he said. "Rush and you might be friends, but him and me gonna kick your ass if you mess this up tonight."

Harv ignored him.

Jimmy crossed the commons to cell three.

At the table Pete played out his hand, then gathered his earnings and entered Harv's cell. He slammed the door shut and grinned at Harv. "Almost lockdown," he said.

The cell was dark and Harv was lying halfway off his mattress on the cold concrete. The water in the toilet ran, and the toilet flushed itself with a whining sound, as it seemed to do every hour or so. He tried to roll over and nearly twisted both ankles; they stuck through the bars at the front of the cell. Light from the hall formed a rhombus on the floor of the commons, pale geometry on a plane crossed with fissures and shadows of the metal table legs. Across the room someone moaned and choked. A voice said, "You keep trying to scream, and we'll keep tightening the rope. Then you can't scream no more. Don't feel very good, does it?"

"You want to choke to death, Willis? That how you want to go?"

"Jimmy's feeling ornery, and he just might strangle you."

"See, we can just string you up, and the guards will call it a suicide."

"You going to be quiet? Ease up, Jimmy. There. Can you breathe now? Good. You ain't going to die, Willis. You're too smart for that. Good boy."

"Now, if you think you can shut up, we might untie you. Think you can keep quiet? Mmm?"

"Don't choke him no more, Jimmy. He's going to be a good boy. Willis don't want to die. Let's get them ropes off."

The silhouette of a guard appeared in the window, shielding his eyes to peer in through the Plexiglas from the bright hallway.

"Shhh," said Rush. "We still got this rope around your neck."

The guard turned and called out something. The lights flashed on in the common room and cells, and the prisoners groaned and turned over on their bunks. Pete sat up, bleary-eyed, and looked around. Harv's eyes hurt, and he closed them. He heard the cell doors swing open.

"Stay in your cells," the guard Neal said.

"Line up and face the wall opposite your bunk," said Bill.

"Okay," said Neal, "what the hell is going on in number three?"

Two men stood with bowed heads, dressed in coveralls; a third was naked, a welt wrung around his skinny neck and a red streak on the inside of one leg.

"Ruschke, number four, face the wall!"

Harv complied. A message was penciled on the wall between two posters in thick, crude lettering: "I can Kill myself if I Want to."

"Has there been a problem in here?" Neal asked.

Rush said, "No, sir."

"Shut up. I'm talking to what's his name, the rapist."

"No."

"Then how come you're crying?"

The cells became sepulchers of laughter.

"Shut up, everyone!" Bill shouted.

"How come?"

"No reason."

A shoe scuffed the concrete. Bill said, "Shit."

"Sauder, come on out here," said Neal. "What the hell are you doing in there?"

"Change of scenery," said Jimmy.

"That so?" said Bill. "Well, let me help you find your way home. Neal, would you hang on to my watch for me? Thanks. Come over here, Jimmy. See, we have our reasons for assigning you to a particular cell. And it angers us when you mess up our system."

Bill wrapped his arm around Jimmy, gesturing with his other hand, and ushered him across the room. But he tripped Jimmy and smashed him headlong into the bars of number four. The bars clanked.

"Oops. He slipped."

"Clumsy. Let's help him up, guys."

The guards raised Jimmy. Vivid blood trickled from his nose and parted around his upper lip, and swelling bloated one socket. His head hung to his chest, and droplets fell from his nose and spattered the shoes of the guards.

"Damn," Bill said with genuine regret. "He's out cold." He rammed his knee into the prisoner's tailbone, and Jimmy's head clanged against the bars. Then Bill hooked his hands in Jimmy's armpits and dragged him into the cell, across Harv's mattress, and tossed him on the bunk.

Neal said, "Ruschke, you seem mighty interested in all this."

"Maybe it's because he's a karate expert. Master of noon chucks. He's looking for pointers."

"You want pointers?"

Harv said nothing. His skin prickled. He did not speak.

A hot, dank voice said in his ear, "Good boy. He might be Curious George, but he knows when to shut his fucking trap."

Harv jammed his elbow backward and caught the guard in the solar plexus. "Goddamn you," he said.

Then his face slammed against the wall, and his nose broke and smeared a bloody print on the concrete. Harv tried to whirl around, but the guards seized his arms and threw their shoulders into his body and pinned him to a slick blur of a girl in panties and bra.

"Smart-ass, eh?"

"What did he say?"

They held him up by the armpits, and a guard slugged both fists in Harv's kidneys.

"Fucking bastard."

"Is that what he said?"

"Shit, I don't know. Ask Bill when he stops wheezing on the ground."

They turned Harv around and beat him and kneed him in the groin as he doubled over, gasping to fill his tight lungs with air, thinking, I will not black out. God help me.

He was conscious. Fists battered his torso and ribs. Harv

flexed his belly to protect himself internally. A stray knuckle grazed the cartilage of his larynx.

Pete was standing, peripherally blind, head bowed and forehead against the wall, which his wisps of chin whiskers brushed. They had stopped.

"He's had enough."

"You learned your lesson?" Bill asked.

"Let him go."

The guards released him, and Harv slumped to the floor, tearing with him a page of thin magazine paper, which drifted back and forth and settled on his chest. The page depicted the faces of a man and a bejeweled woman lacking only a ring through her nose. Across the page was printed:

G   O   L   D
G   O   L   D
G   O   L   D

etc. The bars slammed closed along the walls of the common room, then the hallway door slammed.

Pete squatted beside Harv. "You all right?" he asked. "Look at you—and Jimmy too. This cell is like a casualty ward. Why did you have to sass them? You can't never win with guards and cops, anyway."

Harv rolled onto his mattress. Shreds of tobacco stuck to his cheek.

Pete said, "How you doing?"

"Okay."

When Harv regained his breath, he arose and washed his face in the sink atop the toilet unit. Pete asked, "What did you say to them?" Harv dabbed wet toilet paper at his nose. The water stung, and the paper came away pink.

Pete climbed onto his bunk.

"Some dudes always learn the hard way," he said. "I don't

mean that personally, but you can't get away with smart-assing them deputies. They may be bastards and we know it, but the fact is, we don't got freedom of speech in this joint."

Harv knelt on his mattress and rolled up his blanket to use as a pillow. Pete said, "It's always best to shut up." Harv looked at him, and Pete shut up.

Harv lay on his mattress and tilted his head back to stop the flow of blood down his lip, though this way it drained in his sinuses and tasted like iron. He pressed a wet wad of paper to his nose, which was probably broken, and stared at the toilet upside down. The lights went out. It took his vision a moment to restore the shape of the toilet, like a ventilator on the ceiling of a coffeeshop kitchen.

The room was quiet, except for the muffled sound of Willis sobbing in the dark.

A toe prodded Harv's foot, and a silhouette said, "Rush! Which one of you guys is Harv Rush?" A flashlight shone in his eyes.

"Huh?"

"Are you Rush?"

"Ruschke."

"Key?" The flashlight disappeared behind a clipboard. "Oh, Ruschke. Right. Gather your things and come on out."

Harv wadded up his blanket, put on his plastic slippers, and grabbed a package of cigarettes from the floor, probably Jimmy's. He followed the guard to the glare of the hall lights.

"Jeez," said the guard, raising two fingers toward Harv's face. "What happened to your nose? Was there a fight this evening?"

"No, that happened before my arrest."

"You've got yourself a couple of mean shiners."

"I'm not surprised." The guard handcuffed Harv, who yawned and asked, "What's going on?"

"You're out of here. We're setting you free."

"What do you mean?"

"You're gone from this place. We're releasing you. This jail is too crowded to keep holding minor offenders."

"Is someone taking me back to the Valley?"

"Sorry. You're on your own. We're not running a shuttle service here."

"Hey, wait a second. How am I supposed to get back out there at—what time is it, anyway?"

"Two-thirty. And I don't know. Don't you have any friends you can call?"

"Can I use your phone?"

"Nope. There's a phone booth right down the street."

Harv stripped at the desk and turned in his coveralls. The guard handed him his clothes, along with a cotton T-shirt marked with an emblem and the letters AWPPW. "This isn't mine," he said and tossed the shirt to the guard. The deputy said, "It was in your bag," tossing it back. Harv slipped on the T-shirt.

Harv stood at an intersection of two broad, empty, brightly lit boulevards. Newspapers blew wraithlike on the opposite sidewalk. He could not see a phone booth. It was cold, and he shoved his hands in his pockets and set off walking toward what looked like a gas station sign. Vandals had smashed out the sign's center, Harv saw as he approached, so that it was only an O elevated on a giant pole, ringed in jagged plastic, encircling a mote of the burnt sienna sky. There was a phone booth. Its door was missing, and a bum slept inside with his arms around his knees. The streets were damp and the air smelled like rain, though the sky seemed clear now; the bum must have taken shelter from the rain.

Harv nudged him with his toe. "Hey, beat it. Go sleep on the courthouse lawn." The bum snored on. "Hey, old man, I need to use the phone." Harv shrugged, reached over the bum for the receiver, and dialed the number.

"Hello?"

"Hey, babe. This is Harv."

"Harv! What are you doing?"

"Did Grandpa tell you I was in jail?"

"Yes, he called me this evening. Where are you? Are you phoning from jail?"

"No, they let me out."

"You're kidding! That's wonderful. What time—Harv, it's close to three A.M."

"Yeah, I couldn't believe it. I asked them to keep me till morning, but they refused."

"Where are you?"

"Downtown."

"You mean like downtown LA?"

"Yes." He gave her the intersection.

"You mean they just turned you out on the streets at this hour?"

"Yep."

"I'll get there as fast as I can."

"Thanks. Hurry."

"I will."

Harv paced in front of a concrete island that had rust marks and pipe holes where the gas pumps had stood. Headlights came into the station. A Mercedes-Benz rolled to a stop, and a man wearing green-rimmed sunglasses cranked down his window.

"Need a lift?"

Harv folded his arms. "Piss off."

The driver smiled weakly, rolled up his window, and backed out into the street, wheels screeching. A van swerved to avoid him and blasted its horn. The Mercedes sped off.

Three chicanos were walking up the street, and Harv reached for his pocket, then realized he did not have his switchblade, thinking, Fucking cops—they're supposed to prevent crime, not turn you out on the street in the middle of the night without any damn protection. One of the men told a joke, and they laughed. As they passed the gas station they noticed Harv and fell silent. They were middle-aged, and one had a limp. He kept glancing back at Harv.

Forty minutes later, Harv cleared his throat and rubbed his arms and realized he was catching a cold. A barefoot beggar approached, dressed in two pairs of pants, a sports shirt, and two polyester jackets, and asked Harv for a buck. Harv said no, but the bum persisted until Kristi drove up. Harv said, "I already told you to forget it," but the bum turned and fled the headlights. Harv tried the door on the passenger side of the car, but it was locked. Kristi leaned her elbow on the passenger seat, so that the collar of her V-neck sweater sagged open and Harv saw her breasts beneath the wool, and raised the lock button. He got in and slammed the door and locked it. He wound down the window.

They embraced. Harv stroked her messy hair, and she clung to him.

"Are you all right?"

"Yes, I'm fine."

"Oh, look at your face. What happened?"

"Nothing."

"It looks terrible. Did you get in a fight?"

"Not really. I'll tell you about it later. It doesn't hurt that bad, anyway."

"Let me see your nose."

"Ow! Please don't touch it. Let's get out of here."

As she glanced over her shoulder and pulled away from the curb, Kristi said, "Aren't you cold?"

Harv rolled the window halfway up. "I need some air."

He slid over to sit beside her, resting his feet on the hump in the floor. He wrapped his arm around her shoulders, and with his other hand he stroked the soft front of her sweater, which was at first colorless and then suddenly pink in the glow of a stoplight. She said, "Harv, I'm trying to drive." He rested his head on her shoulder, and she kissed the top of it. "Are you tired?" she asked. Harv said, "Yes." They drove on, and in the brightening and fading luminescence of the street-lamps, Harv saw a tear cross her jawline and trickle down her throat. His eyes stung, and he blinked.

Kristi's muscles worked under his face as she turned the steering wheel and rounded the corner by an all-night pan-cake house. She sniffed and wiped her eyes.

"At least you're free," she said.

"At least," said Harv.

Other Iowa Short Fiction Award Winners

1985
Dancing in the Movies,
Robert Boswell
Judge: Tim O'Brien

1984
Old Wives' Tales,
Susan M. Dodd
Judge: Frederick Busch

1983
Heart Failure, Ivy Goodman
Judge: Alice Adams

1982
Shiny Objects, Dianne Benedict
Judge: Raymond Carver

1981
The Phototropic Woman,
Annabel Thomas
Judge: Doris Grumbach

1980
Impossible Appetites,
James Fetler
Judge: Francine du Plessix Gray

1979
Fly Away Home, Mary Hedin
Judge: John Gardner

1978
A Nest of Hooks, Lon Otto
Judge: Stanley Elkin

1977
The Women in the Mirror,
Pat Carr
Judge: Leonard Michaels

1976
The Black Velvet Girl,
C. E. Poverman
Judge: Donald Barthelme

1975
*Harry Belten and the
Mendelssohn Violin Concerto,*
Barry Targan
Judge: George P. Garrett

1974
*After the First Death There Is
No Other,* Natalie L. M. Petesch
Judge: William H. Gass

1973
The Itinerary of Beggars,
H. E. Francis
Judge: John Hawkes

1972
The Burning and Other Stories,
Jack Cady
Judge: Joyce Carol Oates

1971
*Old Morals, Small Continents,
Darker Times,*
Philip F. O'Connor
Judge: George P. Elliott

1970
The Beach Umbrella,
Cyrus Colter
Judges: Vance Bourjaily
and Kurt Vonnegut, Jr.